DELIVERY

A cautionary tale.

A job, in itself, is not enough.

1

I was twenty-three years old, lacking any sense of direction, stuck on the dole, awaiting a place on the latest poxy government scheme. Life was full of pros and cons. The hours were good but the pay was pathetic. Being a lounge lizard wasn't enough. I ached to have more fun.

I still hadn't managed to find a job. What was wrong with me? Where had I failed? I had potential, bags of the stuff, but how on earth was I going to fulfil it? Crime was not an option as the consequences were severe. Selling my body had sounded good but few would have it free of charge. I'd had a reasonable education but qualifications weren't enough. I needed to find myself a vocation but didn't know where to look.

Eric Peagerm was a lost young man.

I was sat watching afternoon telly. A gardening show. What use was that? I lived upstairs in a council flat and therefore didn't have a garden and didn't subscribe to the house plant ethic as buildings were meant to keep nature *out*. Still, parallels could be drawn, I seemed to be vegetating somewhat, welded firmly to the settee, sat there like a human cabbage.

The gardening show dragged on and on, but the other three channels were more mind-numbing, so consequently I persevered, in case I missed something dramatic. Which I realised was extremely unlikely, these shows rarely had much spice, they'd just been rambling on about rhubarb and now some affable elderly type was asking for some help with his leeks. He stood there in his waterproofs, in a studio, he *did* need help. Had he ever seen the show? They rarely ever left the couch! The expert was more sensibly dressed, in casual slacks and comfortable shoes, he seemed much more at ease with the world, at least until he lurched forward and barked: "ALRIGHT, WHAT'S THE PROBLEM, OLD CHAP?"

Heart trouble, if you're not careful, I thought.

"Well," said the old man, visibly shaken, calming himself by fondling a leek, "I'd like to have a bit more girth . . ."

"Wouldn't we all?" I said out aloud.

"I've asked my peers for advice," he added, "but *their* suggestions haven't helped."

No surprises there, I thought. Even gardeners feared competition.

"So, you'd like more substance for your cock-a-leekie soup?" asked the expert.

"No, I don't care much for leeks . . ."

"GROW SOME BLOODY SPUDS THEN!" I groaned.

Stupidity bothered me, everything did, yet his was nothing compared to mine. I was stuck at home in a wasteland, jobless, hopeless, devoid of dignity. Worse, I was hurling abuse at the telly. This is no way to live, I thought. The world was full of opportunity, countless folk had seized the day, but they'd been lucky, they'd been focussed. Me? I was awash with confusion. While my old schoolmates were out there, plundering the fruits of the earth, I was stumped by the endless possibilities, meanwhile the clock ticked steadily on.

I dragged myself up and walked to the window. Nothing doing. Never was. Slate-grey rooftops stretched out before me, plumes of smoke from the soot-blackened chimney pots only increasing the gloom of the skies. It was the middle of June for Christ's sake, where the hell was the sun? I thought. Too much sun was bad for your health, but none at all was extremely depressing.

Then, through all the despondency, I thought I heard a sound below. Someone knocking on a door . . . *yes* . . . there it was again. I looked and saw a portly fellow, standing in a bungalow doorway, draped in a big brown overcoat with a rather dapper trilby hat. And he wasn't alone. At his side was an odd little figure, stood in a hunch, with beady eyes and protruding teeth, he looked just like a hungover rat. A leather briefcase stood on the floor. It looked like they were selling something. God, perhaps? Why pick on the pensioners, surely *they* would have found him by now? Whoever they were, before too long they'd tramped up the stairs and had found *my* door. Whatever they had I didn't want, but at least these two could answer me back.

"Good afternoon, Sir," said the man in the hat, tipping the brim as he beamed me a smile. "I see you have a graffiti problem."

"Do I?"

"Yes, the corridor walls."

"Well," I started, "kids today have no respect for anything, see?"

"Oh, you're right," agreed his companion, "still, have you ever thought why?"

"No, not really," I replied, "it's just the way things are these days. Blame the parents, not the kids. They're the ones that brought them up."

"I'm sure you're right," said Hat Man, nodding, "these indeed are troublesome times. Nevertheless we're here today to deliver a heartfelt message of *hope*. There are things . . ."

I began to get bored. "Of course there are!" I interrupted. "Sex and drugs and rock 'n' roll, *to hell* with troublesome times, *I* say! The world's a mess, it always was, you've gotta make the best of it, so let the kids blow off some steam and let's *all* have a bit of fun!"

The dynamic duo were taken aback, *that* wasn't anywhere in the script, but soon enough they regained their composure and soldiered on to preach The Truth. 'The Lord Is Our Shepherd' and all that jazz. My soul, apparently, was in danger. They went on and on until I began to yearn for the gardening show! I'd heard enough self-righteous ramblings, *no-one* told me what to do. If anyone had all the answers, surely they'd have a sliver of proof? The Lord had lost me as a child, I'd suffered the deeds of 'Christian' men, I'd also suffered Sunday School, a fountain of hypocrisy. It all came rushing back to me, the emptiness of those sacred rooms, I'd often felt the presence of God but rarely anywhere near a church. They were run by insane old men, unable to answer a reasonable question, twisting the words of holy books to justify their sick little games. Miraculous tales, delivered with gusto, forged to fire young hearts and minds, backed with endless songs of praise which would only encourage their blind obedience. I could see it in their eyes, nothing much had changed, it seemed, and so instead of standing there and swallowing their stupid sermon I set them straight on one or two things and again slammed the door on religion.

BANG!

Then, someone else came knocking. I was not in the mood for guests. However, it was a gentle knock so I leapt up to investigate.

I opened the door to bright blue eyes and a mass of heavenly long, blonde hair. My spirits lifted, briefly, until the old dear who was stood beside her began to deliver the well-worn spiel:

"Good afternoon, Sir," she said with a smile, "I see you have a graffiti problem . . ."

Shit, I thought, *more* of his chosen? Now they were trying the feminine touch.

Grandma was sporting a nice blue rinse, it looked like *she'd* enjoyed a good innings, that gorgeous creature beside her however was sadly squandering her youth. She should've been out having fun in the sun, surely the damn thing was shining somewhere, sampling a few more earthly delights. *I'd* have helped her, that's for sure. It looked like she was still in her teens, with looks like that she could have done anything, yet she was peddling ancient mythology, bible-bashing to any fool who'd listen. Then I considered inviting them in, a heated discussion would pass the time, and perhaps with all my powers of persuasion I'd coax at least one to my own heathen ways? Though it would have been quite a fight, I could have found a purpose in life, to steer the weak away from the light and back towards reality. I suddenly felt like a man with a mission, here was a chance to grab some glory, for a fleeting moment at least, at last my destiny lay before me. Noble as it sounded however I lacked the spirit for such a fight. I did have common sense on my side but women weren't easily dissuaded. Their combined enthusiasm outweighed mine by two-to-one, and anyway, how could a man think straight with much more earthly things on his mind? So, I simply told them the truth, their counterparts had already been round. "I don't need a shepherd," I tried to explain, "I wanna run wild, *far* from the flock. I need no guidance or reassurance in this world *or* the next, alright? I'll take my chances, out with the wolves. Thank you for your time. Goodbye."

"Oh," said grandma.

The girl looked bemused. I gazed at all that beautiful hair. Would *it* become a blue rinse some day? God worked in mysterious ways.

Then another silly fool came rapping. Surely the Lord had accepted defeat? Reluctantly, I got to my feet and made my weary way to the door.

I opened up, expecting the worst, to find Ben Sweeper standing there. Ben was a postman, a middle-aged hippie. Bald but having retained the beard. Despite a decent honours degree he'd somehow drifted into Royal Mail. Had the weed destroyed his ambition? (Though I never smoked and I had none either).

I'd assisted Ben quite often, delivering leaflets on his round. I'd also worked as second auxiliary, down at the sorting office in Statton. Either way the work was easy, simply shoving things through slots, but whereas Royal Mail taxed my wages, Ben would pay me cash-in-hand.

"How's tricks, Ben?" I asked him as he slowly shuffled across the threshold.

"Pissed off, Eric. Same as ever."

That makes two of us, I thought.

"Aye," I told him, "life's a bitch."

He walked across to the window in silence. He just stood there, gazing out. I didn't know what to make of it.

"What's up then, you got more leaflets?"

"No, but look, I might have something." Then he spun around to face me. "Have you any jobs lined up?"

"Come on Ben," I laughed, "you're kidding?"

"No," he said in a serious tone. "There's a full-time job coming up, I thought I'd come and tip you off."

All the despondency melted away. "A full-time job? Christ, at last!" I grabbed a couple of beers from the fridge and cracked them open in celebration.

"So, who's leaving?" I enquired.

"Me," he said, "and any day now; they've signed me up for teacher training, I'll be back at college next month. Anything's better than this," he said, looking down at his well-worn uniform, "University educated and look at the state of me, Eric, just look! I only started out as a temp, until I found a career, y'know, then *fifteen years* flew by," he groaned. "*Fifteen years*, I can't believe it! Alright, so the wages are fair, you barely need to use your brain. All the same I've had enough, so I'm bailing out as soon as I can."

I wasn't so sure what he meant by that and he wouldn't elaborate when I asked. But had enough he most certainly had. That weekend I got a phone call.

"Eric?" It was Edward Thorntree, Supervisor down at Statton. "Could you come in Monday morning? Ben's just had a bit of a turn!"

"Oh?" I told him, feigning surprise. "Aye Ed, you can count on me!"

Maybe he could, maybe he couldn't. Only time would tell on that.

The story was that Ben had snapped, he'd had a blazing row with Ed, who'd constantly been on his back, for turning up late, repeatedly. He only had a ten-minute drive but his cars were always falling apart, and though he had a bike on standby, bikes were nowhere near as fast. At least he *tried* to arrive on time, the whole thing wasn't *entirely* his fault, but Ed was having none of it and he wasn't the only one unhappy. One of his colleagues down at the office had voiced his discontent non-stop, thus Ed had felt the need to act and he'd jumped on Ben at every opportunity. More fool him. Once he had a shiny new career in the pipeline, Ben had hatched a devious plot to get even with the pair of them. He'd left his cigarettes behind on his sorting bench that Friday morning and, since he had an office key, he'd returned that evening to retrieve them. He'd crept in at six o'clock, when Ed was sure to be lurking upstairs, then as he left he'd revved his engine and watched for the twitching curtains. And, sure enough, the following morning, Ed had read the riot act, calling him a 'suspicious type' in front of all of his dumbstruck colleagues. And that was just what Ben had wanted, *he* wasn't giving a whole month's notice, so he'd snapped and gone insane, grabbing all the mail he could find before hurling it into the air, and Ed, amidst a raging whirl of expletives. And when done in the sorting room he'd stomped through to the adjoining shop, where Ed's wife worked behind the screens, and there he'd resumed his scurrilous outburst, ranting and raving as if possessed, letting her know what a husband she had, while she just sat there open-mouthed behind a line of shell-shocked customers.

It was highly amusing of course, but better still, there was now an opening, a rare chance for a job with security, almost unheard of around those parts. Casual work was pleasant enough but a regular wage was far more appealing. Never mind the cash-in-hand, the Mail could tax me all they liked. I wasn't overconfident as full-time jobs were quite elusive, I'd applied the previous year but had been turned down at the interview stage. They'd said I was overqualified. "Isn't everyone?" I'd protested. Not necessarily, they'd implied. I'd find out soon enough.

2

The interviews were finalised, I'd feared a flood of applications. I was wrong, there were only five. Every one of us got an invite. It was rather hard to believe. Had the unemployed lost hope? Roaming the streets at a nice steady pace didn't hold that much appeal, it seemed. Was the early start to blame or the six-day working week, I wondered. Either way, the pay was great for a job I knew was a bit of a doddle.

The assessments were held in Boroughby, fifteen miles or so down the road. Everyone arrived on time and there we sat in the waiting room with an air of apprehension.

It started off with an aptitude test. I couldn't believe how easy it was. Pick the odd-one-out from word groups:

settee   table   sideboard   dog

Sometimes there'd be pictures instead, if anything they were easier, there might be a pig with a curly tail amongst a little group with straight ones. Two of the applicants failed this test. Though surprised, I wasn't amused. Perhaps their lives were less demanding? Maybe they were better off? "I'm just a farm-hand," one of them said. "Not an intellectual." I didn't feel too bright myself, considering why *I* was there.

The other failure was Harry Shaw, he had the part-time round at Statton. Since his wife had just retired he'd felt the need to work more hours. Now, of course, he had *no* chance. Somebody had screwed up somewhere. Twenty years of service and he *still* couldn't meet the basic requirements. Then it emerged that another applicant worked as a full-time postman already. He'd decided to apply as Statton was slightly closer to home. But that wasn't how things worked with Royal Mail, there were regulations to follow. He was informed that he needed a *transfer* and ordered to leave the building at once.

That left only me and Frank, an older, wiry, Statton lad. I knew him from the football field, the Trimley and District Sunday League. This time it was one on one. Who would win today, I wondered? This was quite a different game. Just what attributes were required? Fitness, had that. Honesty, yes. I.Q. above a farm-hand, apparently. Still, I knew that more was required. Time to face the verbal assault.

The interview room looked very familiar, pale blue walls and a threadbare carpet. Sadly, so did the personnel, the same cocky swines that had grilled me the last time. Mr. Charlesworth was in charge, a sour old goat with a manner to match. He'd been hiring and firing there since 1965 or so. His eyes were piercing, big, bushy eyebrows sprang from his head at impossible angles, he would frown with such disdain you'd think he'd swallowed a mouthful of shit. And there he sat, impassively, along with his weasel of a sidekick, gathering his thoughts before he nailed me to the wall again. Not *this* time, old man, I thought, I knew that I could take him on, an endless string of potential employers had toughened me up for the task ahead. Interviews were easy to get, the difficult part was the act that followed, playing the ideal candidate when it was obvious you weren't. It was all about perception, I would have to alter theirs. I sat up straight and listened intently, waiting for the inevitable.

And soon enough it came.

"Hmm, well," said Mr. Charlesworth, scowling at my application, "you have *A-Levels* here, it says, and frankly that concerns me somewhat. Isn't this a tad beneath you? Postal work is fairly simple. Chances are you'd leave us flat for something more appropriate."

I felt a sudden surge of emotion. *Right,* I thought, *you asked for it.* I shuffled forward, took a deep breath and put *him* straight on one or two things.

"Look," I said, "I'm a fit young man, right now I'm twenty-three years old, but *I* left school with honest intent, and all I've heard from the likes of you are two opposing lines of reasoning. One: my A Level grades are poor, those 'D's and 'E's don't count, it seems, and Two: because I dared to *take* them, I'm *beyond* a menial job; now listen, Mr. Charlesworth, I've put up with this for five long years! One failed interview after another! What does it take for a chance these days? I'm already second auxiliary, I'm familiar with the walks, I've had a go on *all* of them and *never* felt superior! You turned me down for this *last* year, it seems you're after a bunch of fools, but *I* have a postman too, y'know, and I'd rather have an intelligent type as opposed to some inadequate retard who couldn't tell his arse from his elbow! Plus, I know a *graduate* who's been a postie for *fifteen years!* The guy who left this very job! So why does it matter that *I'm* no fool?"

I couldn't be sure that I wasn't a fool, but so what, I could do the job backwards. I'd been pretty clear on that, I hadn't paused in the whole damn speech. I did regret my opening line, 'the likes of you' was a bit of a slight, but that was out of sheer frustration, surely they would understand?

Mr C. sat back in his seat and glanced across to his silent assistant. After that it was all pretty standard, basic questions, easy answers.

"Well, Mr. Peagerm," he concluded, shuffling his papers, "you'll be hearing from us in due course. Thank you very much for your time."

And off I trotted, full of beans, feeling rather pleased with myself. I had made a lasting impression, surely that was *more* than enough? I'd been firm, direct, emotive. I had bared my very soul. I'd laid it on the line with passion. How on earth could they refuse?

My speech, however, hadn't mattered. Nor had my experience. Frank had a wife and kids at home and that, it seemed, was more important.

"That guy *needs* it more than you," the doorman told me as I left. "He's got a family at home. Two young boys and a baby girl."

"How do *you* know?" I demanded.

"Oh, we had a little chat. *He* looked like the nervous type, I thought I'd calm him down a bit; but that's the sort of thing they look at, *he'll* be more committed to the cause."

"What cause?"

"Why, the *Postal* cause! The safe delivery of the mail!"

"Oh . . ."

"You're still young, y'see, you're still footloose and fancy-free . . ."

"So?"

"Well . . . lads *your* age are often unreliable."

Unreliable? Hey, not me, I'd never *signed-on* late before, besides, I knew some married men who phoned-in sick at the drop of a hat! No wonder I was unemployed, all they wanted was commitment, yet, according to Royal Mail, single young men couldn't give it. *What a load of crap,* I thought. Had they not been paying attention? I'd been on their books for years and not once had I turned down work. And who'd delivered the morning papers, faithfully, before dashing to school, come rain, hail, sleet or snow, for a measly two-pound-fifty a week? Single lads were full of life, of course we had our freedom, but it wasn't any use to us without a job to complement it. Wasn't this a *physical* job? Surely, fit young folks were needed? Just because we had no ties it didn't mean we weren't committed.

Stick yer job! I thought to myself, I'd had enough of being auxiliary. Who would want to work in a place with shitty attitudes like that? I wasn't about to get strapped with a mortgage, a wife and a couple of kids for a job. Frank could have it if *that's* what it took. I'd gladly take my talents elsewhere.

Thankfully, I didn't have to. Frank had made a fatal mistake. He'd told them of another interview, making out he was in

11

demand. And that'd had the opposite effect, they'd hung around to hear the outcome, and when he was offered *that* job, they'd told him he should snap it up.

I was left without competition. I was a postman by default. Not *that* much to be proud of, but a step in the right direction, at least. Now I didn't need state support I'd start to build some self-esteem. I wouldn't have to sit in limbo, languishing till giro day. At last I'd have a regular wage, life assurance, a pension plan. Now I could begin to live. *To hell* with afternoon TV!

3

Right away they swore me in and measured me up for the uniform. I'd passed the medical as a temp, at least I was spared *one* physical assault. I know they're checking for hernias when they cup your balls and ask you to cough, but all the same it just feels wrong. Surely there's a better way?

The first day on the job was great. Everybody seemed relieved. I knew the drill, I'd been a temp, I didn't need a shred of help. Sticking mail into pigeonholes was child's play with *my* potential, sorting and delivering it were minor complications. I felt at ease with everyone, my workmates were a friendly crew, the only thing that bothered me was why they all seemed so content. Mr Charlesworth had a point, the work was quite repetitive. The same routine, day after day. Didn't it ever get them down? But then I thought about their options: factory work, an office job, shop assistant, cleaner, labourer, few of which were available locally, suddenly it made more sense. I'd also hoped there were hidden pleasures, things they never told the temps, perhaps frustrated middle-aged women would ask me in for gratuitous sex or wealthy widows with fortunes to spare would give me enormous tips at Christmas? Some, it seemed, were still having problems getting to grips with decimal currency, so the whole thing was conceivable, if a bit unlikely.

The sorting office meanwhile was an end-of-terrace property, with living quarters up above and a regular Post Office off to one side. We sorted and delivered mail for Statton, Colton, Grangeworth and Trimley; my walk covered half of Trimley, just a stone's throw from the flat. The area was semi-rural, a loose collection of shabby villages, built in the nineteenth century to facilitate the need for coal. It didn't last. The twentieth century saw the industry in decline and most of the pits had long since closed with precious little to replace them. Little in the way of jobs, the government could hardly care. Thatcher had destroyed the unions, North-East England was suffering. So why hadn't hundreds wanted this job? I still couldn't get my head around it. Granted, more than half the day was spent outside whatever the weather; still, you got to sort the mail in a homely little office space. Homely to a certain degree, the place was warm but rather spartan, four bare walls like sallow skin and a ceiling which had so many cracks it looked like the world's most monotonous jigsaw. Metal frames were screwed to the walls for sorting the mail into separate streets, with sturdy wooden benches below, surrounding a gnarly old sorting table.

Mail came in unprocessed so you had to sort it into walks. Then you sorted into streets. This would take an hour or so. After that you took each street and sorted into delivery order, securing them with elastic bands, which maybe took another hour. Once you'd wrapped your final street you'd stuff the bundles into your pouches, padding them out with larger items, magazines, the occasional packet. Should you be the first to finish, you would offer your assistance. If it wasn't needed you were ready for your walk.

The walks would take a couple of hours, each was of a similar size, one was part-time, four full-time and one was done in the van, (full-time). The part-time walk belonged to Harry, the one who'd failed his aptitude test. Poor old chap, he was fifty-six and pretty much falling apart at the seams. He sat in a heap at his bench each morning, fingers flushed with nicotine stains, coughing up his lungs into a filthy-looking handkerchief. The full-time crew, apart from me, were Sheila, Tony, Kenny and Jack. Full-time meant you did two deliveries (or at least you were supposed to). Sheila was pushing fifty herself but walked as fast as many could run, she seemed to glide on a cushion of air with what appeared to be the minimum effort. Tony was around my age, he also had a Trimley walk. Once we'd finished sorting he would give me a lift in his Ford Cortina. Kenny was a character, a stout little fellow with big, bulging eyes. Not quite Marty Feldman but enough to make you uncomfortable. He'd prowl around with an air of mischief, grinning like a Cheshire cat, then he'd sidle up to you and try to sell you something or other. He served the farms, the rural addresses and business premises using the van, which doubled as a mobile shop, he'd buy and sell whatever was available: free-range eggs, second-hand clothes, fruit and veg, sea coal, the lot. Nevertheless he was always skint. Where his money went was a mystery. He would stand around each morning, fumbling through his pockets for change, then when he found some he'd stare at it, as if it had some mystical quality. He would roll his own cigarettes, his car appeared to run on fumes, the petrol gauge was working but was always close to zero.

And that leaves Jack. Jack Moran. They all disliked him, the office misery. Ben despised him, citing him as the one who'd forced him into teaching. Everyone had warned me that I'd have to watch my back, or else, and though I found that hard to believe since he'd been fine with me in the past, his general disposition did suggest he had a few psychoses. It was something about his eyes, full of fear and repressed animosity, an unusual combination projecting an air of intense paranoia. Still, I was twenty-three and knew that looks could be deceptive. Give the bloke a chance, I thought. Everyone deserved one.

A fortnight passed and my legs were aching, all that walking took its toll. My feet were badly blistered too, I'd never had all this as a temp. No-one had said much out on the streets, they must have thought I was still auxiliary; no-one had asked what had happened to Ben, I just assumed he hadn't been popular. Everyone knew his cars were crap, his clientele included, who'd be left in the lurch on giro day while he was stuck on a back road somewhere, bonnet up, spirits down. I wondered if *I'd* be popular as I soaked up the warmth of the morning sun, roaming the streets like an overgrown paperboy, peaceful, not a care in the world. It was a sleepy summer's morning, hardly anyone up and about, then just as I turned down Monkton View with the lazy sun still low in the sky, I was suddenly met by a scruffy young urchin, munching away on a piece of toast.

"Got any blow?" he asked me abruptly, cheeks all smothered in strawberry jam. 'Blow' was dope as far as I knew. Surely he meant something else?

"Whaddya mean by 'blow'?" I asked.

"I dunno, it's for me dad. 'Go and ask the postman,' he said. I think he puts it in his baccy."

So it was true, the whole thing was true! There were hidden pleasures alright, not only had Ben fleeced the old folks and seen to the needs of middle-aged women, but also he'd sold dope as a sideline! Nip *this* in the bud, I thought.

"Look," I said, "go tell yer dad there's someone different on the post; a big, tall lad who *doesn't sell drugs*, especially to little kids!"

"Whaddya mean?" he asked me, blankly.

"NO MORE BLOODY BLOW, ALRIGHT?"

This was *my* turf now, I thought, and woe to those who crossed me!

4

The hardest part of the job by far was getting to the office on time. The mail came in at 6 a.m. which meant you had to get up at five. Easy when you're sober but a pain if you'd been down the pub. Trimley was a little place. The pubs were all we had.

My stupid alarm clock didn't help, it seemed to have a mind of its own. Had I remembered to set the alarm it hardly ever rang on time, and when it did, that feeble bell would hardly ever wake me up. Even if I heard the bell I'd usually ignore it, or just lie there staring into space, in need of inspiration.

Finally the phone would ring and I'd be forced to answer it. Ed would always sound annoyed.

"Hello? Is that Eric Peagerm?"

"Aye . . . who the hell are you?"

"Don't get wise with me, my lad!"

"Oh, good morning."

"Well?"

"Well what?"

"Are you gracing us with your presence?"

Though I'd still be half asleep at least I would be on my feet. I'd tell him I was on my way, before he got sarcastic.

And I was, in a fashion, though it took an hour to get there, getting dressed was quite a chore and Statton was two miles away. Regardless of my waking state that little stroll would clear my head. Unfortunately, on arrival, I would have another problem. Office lights were far too bright. Hadn't they heard of dimmer switches? I'd be blinded by the glare as I fumbled around to locate my stool. Jack was mad on days like these. Jack, it

17

seemed, was mad full stop. He would stand there moaning and groaning, getting more worked up by the minute. What incensed him was that I had raised his workload by a sixth, or a third if Kenny was late, and that was pretty common too. Jack was alright, he was married. Living proof there's someone for everyone. Getting up was easy for him. I had no such help.

But he *was* a bastard, after all. Jack Moran the union man. He acted like he owned the place and Ed just let him ramble on. He loved to quote the regulations, none of which he followed himself, claiming there was a 'local agreement' that somehow rendered him exempt. He'd recite from this mystical document, signed, he said, before our time. It would change to meet his needs. No-one else had seen a copy.

Soon I got a call from Ed. "Listen, Eric," I was told, "you can't keep sleeping-in like this. Someone's made a formal complaint."

"Jack, you mean."

"Er, well, yes. But he's got a valid point. You'll have to pull your socks up or I'll have to put you on report."

"Look," I said, "I'm young and single, I've a social life, y'know? Getting up at five o'clock just takes a bit of getting used to. I'll adjust, eventually, but meanwhile here's a little thought: why not ring me up each morning, let's say, what, at five-past five?"

"You're joking, right?"

Wrong. "Why not?"

"Eeee, WHY NOT?" he squealed, "WHY NOT? For starters, I'd be still asleep and I'M not getting up for YOU! You've been here a month, if that! Who the hell do you think you are?"

"Right," I countered, "how about ten-past?"

"WHAT?" he gasped. "Are you FOR REAL? Would you like to pay my PHONE BILL?"

What did *that* have to do with it? The phone would ring, I'd crawl from bed, I'd go to work and arrive on time. If I didn't answer the call, it wouldn't have cost him *anything*, right?

Sadly, Ed just couldn't see it. I was getting nowhere fast. He was getting more upset. A new approach was badly needed.

"Look," I told him, "how about this: I'll get a new alarm clock, right? The one I've got's as old as *you*; you can't say fairer than that, OK? But what about the two-mile walk? There's a van outside, y'know. Maybe you could ask our Kenny to come and pick me up each morning?"

"Ah," he said, "I thought of that but what about when *he* sleeps-in? And when I asked him all he said was 'it's a post van not a taxi'!"

What a bloody cheek, I thought, he used that van as a mobile shop! Ed was well aware of that. They must have shared the profits. Thus I cornered Kenny the following day who said they had indeed discussed it, though he claimed it was *his* idea and it was Ed that wasn't keen.

"A liar, huh?"

"Well, y'see, he's not a very trusting sort, he thought that if you had a lift you just might sleep-in all the more."

Lovely, that was all I needed, I had *two* of them against me. In a disciplinary case I knew I wouldn't stand a chance. Unions were a waste of time, support from colleagues seemed unlikely. If deception was his game I'd simply have to strengthen mine.

Yet I'd made a solemn promise. I was always loath to break them. I screwed up occasionally but still retained my principles. And so I got my notepad out and wrote a little shopping list:

> Beer
> Food
> Bog Roll
> Clock

Nothing fancy, just essentials. Ed could bullshit all he wanted, I preferred the honest approach. *I* could get to sleep at night. If only getting up was as easy.

5

Pay days were miraculous, like giro day with an extra zero. Every night I'd swill it down and rarely came home less than slaughtered. Dole queue nights had been depressing, little left once bills were paid. Gut-rot cider or cut-price cans were all I could afford back then. There'd been one eventful year when home brew was the latest thing, but all that madness had to stop, the hangovers were horrible and the yawning gaps in my recollection were worrying to say the least. Plus, the girls were less than impressed by a slobbering wreck without a real job. I rarely had a love life but on home brew it was out of the question. Now I had a steady income I could drink with more refinement, beer was tasting good again, the flat no longer smelled like a brewery. Fewer people came by but I saw enough of them down the pub. I'd become a man of means. I was walking with a swagger.

And it felt as though I knew things, what exactly wasn't clear, it curiously started when I signed the Official Secrets Act. I was handling sensitive material, some of it extremely personal, plain brown envelopes stuffed with pornography, dildos, butt plugs, nipple clamps, the lot! Maybe that's why folk were friendly, keep the postman loyal and true? Once I could get up in the mornings, I was going to love this job. Yes, there was a uniform but they were issued free of charge. I hated spending cash on clothes when I realised how many pints it cost. Anyway, where *was* that uniform, couldn't they find one in my size? I was over six feet tall but that was hardly exceptional.

Meanwhile I performed my duties in my regular attire, shirt and shorts if the weather was good, jeans and a scruffy old coat if not. I got a more reliable clock, which got me out of bed most days, though never on a Saturday when a major earthquake wouldn't have roused me. I'd be laid there, catatonic, Friday nights were spent on the town, I'd drink until the early hours with scant regard for things like work. Of course, I'd be hopelessly late, that I arrived at all was amazing, Ed's harsh words had worked to a point but weekends were a special case. Kenny on the other hand seemed to sleep-in twice a week at least. Why, I never understood, he didn't drink as far as I knew. He'd roll in forty minutes late, unwashed, unshaven, hair in a mess, his shoelaces and shirt and undone, his big bug-eyes reduced to slits in froglike mounds of swollen flesh. Between us we had poor old Jack in a constant state of irritation, he would stand there shaking his head while mumbling profanities under his breath. Office banter became quite strained. Conversations would end abruptly. Jack would always interject with every statement dripping with sarcasm.

Kenny soon got sick of this and captured Ed one afternoon, eventually persuading him to authorise the taxi run. Saturdays only, initially, but overall it was better than nothing. *You* try walking a couple of miles after thirteen pints and two hours sleep. I knew exactly what Kenny was up to, he was a crafty little sod, his angle was that, should he succeed, they might just overlook the fact that *his* shortcomings were worse than mine. And being a martyr wasn't so bad, he wouldn't have to use *his* car, and at least he wasn't stuck in the office with Jack and Ed's moronic chatter.

So, Saturdays improved, I had a chauffeur all of my own, what dragged me out of bed though was the dreaded sound of the entrance buzzer. Each flat block had an outer door, and though those doors were rarely locked, the buzzers worked around the clock and the sound would make you grind your teeth. You know that board game, *Operation?* Crank it up a thousand times. Just as jarring, just as annoying and Kenny wouldn't let it go until I'd scrambled across to the intercom.

Once I'd made it down the stairs I'd clamber into the waiting van and relate what had happened the previous night, assuming that I could remember, if not I'd be told about the best of the farmers' wives that week, delightful, one and all it seemed and at least one would have been buck naked. Finally we'd reach the office, where I'd have a raging thirst. I'd sit there with a water bottle, sucking on it furiously. Once I used a vodka bottle, just to see what Jack would say. He didn't say a thing that day. Everybody thanked me. But it wasn't easy sorting mail, being tall, tired and therefore unbalanced, I would have to widen my stance to stop myself from toppling over. Which in turn had repercussions, beer-drenched farts would often escape, and though they never made much sound they stank like something had died up there. Each time I unleashed a gust I found it impossible not to laugh, while everybody else around me coughed and spluttered, helplessly. Jack complained to Ed of course but he couldn't declare it a fart-free zone as Kenny, Harry, Jack and himself were smoking cigarettes in there. "That's pollution too," I told them, "not to mention the risk of fire." I had them by the balls and they knew it. I was learning fast. Plus, I wasn't the only one letting them fly, Kenny lived on a diet of beans, and Tony liked a beer or two, especially on Friday nights. The farting flowed so freely in there that Sheila suggested we get some gas masks. Kenny said he'd make enquiries. Nothing seemed beyond his grasp.

Out on the streets the air would improve but soon the hangover would hit me. Humping heavy bags of mail was hardly what a drinker needed. If it was cold, wet or windy the force of the elements kept me going; if it was warm and sunny however my head would be throbbing, mercilessly. My clothing would be drenched in sweat, those Saturdays were unrelenting, every street seemed longer than usual, meanwhile they'd be full of my people, dazzling me with wit and charm.

"Where the hell were *you* last night?"

"Cheer up, it's a lovely day!"

"At least it's better than walking the streets!"

Comedians, the lot of 'em.

Whatever the weather, the afternoon would be spent on the couch or back in bed. Then as six o'clock approached I'd gear up for the Saturday night. Followed by Sunday morning football, twenty-two men in a hell of a state, running around, kicking lumps out of anything that moved within range. After that we drank in The Stag. Usually, well into the night, providing nobody stepped out of line and managed to get us all evicted.

There was one such Sunday at the end of a warm but cloudy summer. Terry Bell, a mate of mine, was caught red-handed by the landlord pissing into one of his plant pots. Terry was a rascal, but a funny one, so you forgave him. As a team we backed him so we all got turfed out into the rain.

All the other pubs were shut, they locked the doors at three back then. "Fuck it," I said, "I need some sleep," and I tramped off home to find my bed.

I couldn't remember hitting the pillow but woke to the sound of the telephone ringing. How long had I been asleep? The clock was reading five-past six. I got to my feet as quick as I could, got washed and dressed and left for work. I crossed the main road, dodging the puddles and headed off down Statton Lane.

Presently, a trashed old Jeep pulled up beside me with a screech. It was Soapy Joe, a drunk. I seemed to know a lot of those. Though I knew that it was risky, I was tired and rather late, and thus I struggled with the door and gratefully accepted the lift.

"Where ya gannin' kid?" he asked me, louder than was necessary, stale tobacco on his breath with overtones of the cheapest whiskey.

"Doin' awatime?"

"Shit, I hope not, far too knackered for *that* game, Joe!"

"Basic hours for a basic wage! All a fella needs!"

"Right! What about you? Where ya headed?"

"Offta the pub!"

"Bloody hell! Who serves beer at six in the mornin'?"

"*Mornin'? That's* a lang way off!"

I stopped to consult my brain for a moment. *Hmm, yes, he was probably right.* "One of us is daft," I said, "and chances are it isn't you!"

He chuckled as he hit the brakes then cackled as we ground to a halt. I struggled with the door again then stepped out into a pool of water. "Shit!" I groaned as I slammed the door. Joe just sat there, pissing himself. I turned around and tramped off home, annoyed, embarrassed and wet.

Next I knew the alarm went off. The clock said it was just gone five. Nevertheless, just to be sure, I thought I'd check it out on Teletext.

05:02 / Mon / Aug 30.

Good, it was safe to get up. There was even time for a bath so I quickly set the taps in motion.

Afterwards I made some coffee and dragged some dry shoes out of the cupboard. Then I had a shave, got dressed and set off right on schedule.

I had my head on straight, at last. I finally knew what I was doing. The sun was rising, there, in the east, exactly where it should have been.

I got to the office at five-to six to find the front door firmly locked. Ed had slept-in for a change. *I* could act superior now. I turned around and sat on the steps and watched the rabbits in the field. *They* didn't have to work hard, they just nibbled at plant stems and humped each other senseless.

After a while I checked my watch. Ten-past six. Where were the others? I pressed my ear against the door . . . nothing . . . not the slightest sound. I clambered up and crossed the road and looked up at the bedroom window. Nothing doing, the curtains were drawn. This was *most* unusual. The streets were eerily silent too. Where was everyone this morning? Where was the traffic? Where were the people? Why wasn't anyone going to work?

Finally, it dawned on me. Even *we* didn't work Bank Holidays. *Jesus Christ,* I thought to myself. *What the hell's the matter with me?* I mulled it over briefly then decided it was Terry's fault. It seemed a long walk home that day. I prayed that no-one saw me.

6

Edward Thorntree, Supervisor. He was in a class apart. His lower lip hung down on his chin and his balding, undersized head seemed to follow, giving him an ape-like posture which complemented his flat-footed gait. He had a story for every occasion and made great efforts to repeat them. One about a butcher's van was aired at least on a weekly basis. Having previously owned a pub we guessed those tales were gleaned from the bar. We caught him out on details but he rambled on regardless.

Sometimes I was first one in and that's when *I* caught most of his rubbish. When he had you on your own you really wished you'd stayed in bed. For example, during the night, I'd often have to take a leak, and if it was after 4 a.m. I might get dressed and set off early. On arrival, Ed would be stood there, changing the date stamps or reading the paper or combing his sideburns over his head, in order to look ridiculous.

"Scrivens!" he'd say. "Wet the bed?"

"Not since last week's bestial orgy."

He would always seem unmoved. Still, I liked to keep him guessing.

Then he'd try one-upmanship. "Have you ever *killed* an animal?"

"That depends. Are *humans* animals?"

"No."

"Alright. The answer's 'no' then."

I'd be hoping he'd retort so I could think of more scenarios, sadly he would rarely bite and off he'd go with his own agenda:

"Well, I worked in a slaughterhouse once, up to our *waists* in blood we were, it all congealed around your hands and it was *torture* scrubbing it off . . ."

At this point I'd be tearing my hair out. Where the hell was everyone else? Then he'd show me his middle finger, the one he couldn't seem to bend. "That's arthritis, that," he'd tell me, holding it up against the light. His initials were E.T. We got some mileage out of that one!

"Jimmy Jones," he'd ramble on, "made walking sticks from donkeys' dicks . . . Joey Jones, or was it Johnny . . . ?"

"Jacky," I'd say.

"That's right, Jacky! Anyway, we were in the army, 1952 I think . . ."

Then Kenny might wander in to save me.

"Christ, *another one* wet the bed?"

Kenny wouldn't say a word, he'd look towards me, knowingly, then snatch the van keys from the hook and slither off outside.

"So, where was I?" Ed would ask.

"Oh, you'd finished," I'd reply, or maybe if I had the munchies, "something about a bacon sandwich?"

Finally the rest would arrive and Jack would always have a pop. "What's the matter? Couldn't sleep?"

"Nah. Nightmares. *You* were in 'em."

Now and then I'd catch a lift from someone who had been on night shift, that would make me early too, but only when the weather was good. Few would have you sat in their cars when all your clothes were soaking wet. I didn't care, I walked for a living. Ed could torture someone else.

Cars meanwhile were Kenny's passion, he was always on about them. "Pass your driving test," he'd tell me, "then I'll fix you up with something." He'd acquire these battered old wrecks then weld them up with pieces of scrap, and should one pass its MOT, he'd always manage to palm it off on some poor soul he'd met on his rounds. The MOTs themselves were a farce, Kenny liked to take a chance, but he would take them like no-one else and Tony gave me a few examples.

An inspector stood in the pit beneath one of Kenny's improbable creations, poking around with a tip of a bradawl, risking life and limb in the process. "What's this *handle* for?" he'd asked while making sure the floor was solid. It was part of an old fridge door that Kenny had used as a makeshift patch. Another time the inspector's hand had plunged right through the floor of the car. Somebody had patched it up with a copy of the Daily Mirror. Kenny of course denied all knowledge and claimed that he'd been sold a ringer. The inspector had his doubts, considering it was that day's paper.

I just had a provisional licence. I could drive, in a fashion, but in order to pass my test I needed more experience. My dad had taught me how to drive but mostly worked away from home and, since he knew me well enough, he'd always take the car keys with him. Then, one morning, quite by chance, I came across some information, Royal Mail had a driving scheme, they got you through the test for free.

Kenny told me all about it. "Just ask Ed to sort it out."

"Would you, Ed?"

"Well, I could, but who am I supposed to ask?"

Surprisingly, Jack piped up, "Ring Bob Ross at Regional Office. *He's* in charge of the driving scheme, his number's in the office handbook."

That was somewhat out of character, Jack the Bastard offering help. Self-preservation, I was told, I even got an explanation.

Should I manage to pass my test they'd train me up to cover the van. Tony covered it as it stood but only Jack could cover Tony. Jack however wasn't keen so this was a golden opportunity, once I'd got myself a licence, I'd slot in as second cover and he'd be allowed to stick to his walk.

That didn't make any sense at first. What was wrong with driving duty? Vans were warm and carried the weight and made the job a lot less tiring. Kenny explained: "One time there were three of us who shared the driving, one retired then another got sacked so I was left without any cover. Ben had only just came in and Tony wasn't here back then. Sheila was a pedestrian, so I was asked to train our Jack."

And what wonderful training he gave him.

There was a farm on Latchworth Lane with a vicious Doberman on patrol, which suddenly bounded out from the barn as Jack was sliding the mail through the door. He'd almost made it back to the van but the door wouldn't open, mysteriously, and the dog had chased him around the yard while Kenny just sat with a devilish grin.

So, with Jack's incessant reminders, Ed enquired about the driving. Sadly I had a six-month wait as I was merely there on approval. New recruits got twelve months probation, everybody had to endure it. I was barely halfway through. I hadn't even made it to Christmas. But that Christmas came and went, generally without much fuss, the volume of mail increased threefold but the smaller things were most problematic. Around that time, the general public simply couldn't remember addresses. According to those Christmas cards, Mrs Moore of Raby Road could have lived at No.2, or 3, or 23, or anywhere! Some couldn't even remember the street: "*The little street behind the pub, across the road from the big white house . . .*" Which pub, *which* bloody big white house? The whole thing drove me up the wall! I was still comparatively new, I didn't know where *everyone* lived, and Mrs Moore could have popped her clogs but the cards kept flooding in regardless.

Meanwhile I'd expected tips. Someone said I'd double my wages. Someone lied. Kenny meanwhile got lots of lovely things from the farmers: chickens, turkeys, bottles of spirits, sacks of potatoes, a sweater or two. Most of the others did reasonably well, except for Jack, who didn't get anything. Jack was a bastard and *everyone* knew. His customers knew, his kids both knew. I had to assume if his good wife knew, she didn't have the sense to leave him. I got a fiver to help me through college. Somebody thought I was seasonal help. Those wealthy widows I'd hoped for must have been on someone else's walk. Not that I was too upset, Christmas was a lucrative season, overtime in a satellite office had nothing to do with working over. Ed would simply sign those sheets no matter how many hours we claimed. The longer we were 'working' meant the longer he was 'supervising'.

7

Soon enough a year had passed. Time for my probation review. Only one thing really mattered: had my performance been acceptable? That was largely up to Ed, that paragon of virtue, but although he wasn't my number one fan, he hadn't been keeping appropriate records or sending in punctuality reports. Any sudden criticism now would have needed additional justification. Lacking proof, his hands were tied. It looked like he was stuck with me.

So, Head Office sent a suit to stamp me with their seal of approval. When he arrived he scowled at me. It didn't *look* like he approved.

"Where's your uniform, Mr Peagerm?"

"You tell me," I told him. "I was only measured a year ago. Perhaps we need to wait a while?"

He glanced at Ed who gave him the nod, then turned to me with a look of embarrassment. "Right then," he conceded, "I'll get onto stores this afternoon."

"Thanks," I said, "whenever you can." I was not in any hurry. Summer was upon us, I was happy wearing t-shirts.

My first encounter with the bosses. They were from a different world. Still, I'd passed their little test and so to celebrate, after work, I spent the rest of the week in the pub. Afternoon *and* evening sessions. Chip shop visits in between. A simple life, a good one, if a little wearing on the system. Plus, I slept-in every day without a word from Jack or Ed. The future looked increasingly bright. And now I had those driving lessons.

Learning to drive in a Royal Mail vehicle simplifies the whole equation; as it's free there's nothing to lose, it's someone else's car and insurance. My advice to youngsters is apply to Royal Mail straight from school, then pass your driving test, resign, and find a job that's more rewarding. Had *I* had such good advice it could have saved a lot of trouble. Not that I'd have listened then. I was quite content with things.

The driving I found quite relaxing, my instructor was excellent, and soon enough I was full of confidence, rush hour traffic couldn't faze me. After a week of solid practice I sat the test the following Monday, which I passed with consummate ease, breezing through like a seasoned pro. At last I was a qualified driver, after years of L-plate misery. One more hurdle had been cleared. I was making steady progress.

And they didn't waste much time, they stuck me in the van at once. Kenny was going to show me the ropes while somebody else assumed my walk. I presumed it would be easy, I'd be chauffeured around at leisure, which to some extent was true but I soon found many skills were needed.

I'd been there a year or so with relatively little drama, I'd performed without much fuss, but therein lay a growing problem. Nothing had got my adrenaline flowing, I didn't have any stories to tell, no sex-starved housewives had seduced me, I hadn't been terrorised by a dog. The postal life was becoming a bore, I didn't even look the part, but maybe that was it, I thought, could a uniform make all the difference? Kenny didn't think so, he suggested I pay more attention. *He* said there were opportunities. Opportunities? What did he mean? Granted, on an average day I roamed the streets in a bit of a daze, but even when my head was clear I saw no opportunities. *He* was like a travelling salesman, out of sight along dusty farm tracks. I had my pouches, myself and the streets. What was *I* supposed to do?

"It doesn't matter," he insisted, "*go seek out* the opportunities, learn exactly who lives where, what they've got and what they can spare. Smile a lot. Ask how they're doing.

Show them you're a man they can trust. A regular smile should get you the spare, and with a bit of charm, who knows?"

"What do *they* get, in return?"

"Well," he said, "there's peace of mind. Pay attention to the mail. Discretion has some value, right?"

I knew exactly what he meant but that was only half the story. Some things I would have to learn, some I didn't want to know. I was quite naive at times, some were *very* friendly, but I took it with a pinch of salt, I never dreamed of taking advantage. Growing up I'd been quite distant, I'd been shy and insecure, my conversational skills were lacking, my social awareness pitifully poor. I'd spent too much time alone and when I wasn't I'd be drunk. Maybe it was high time I began to take some notice?

We pulled into the boarding kennels, half a mile down Statton Lane. Barking echoed through the courtyard. No place for a couple of postmen.

"Come on Kenny," I demanded, "let's have all the dirt on Ed."

"Well, if you must," he sighed, sinking backwards into his seat. "Right, y'know that little corner, over by the overtime sheets?"

"Aye."

"Well, that's 'Wankers Corner'. Ed was standing there one day with his trousers down and his todger out."

"*That's* the reason why you groan whenever you're doing your overtime sheets?"

"Right."

"I couldn't work it out, I just thought you were losing it!"

"He gives me money every month to buy him mucky magazines. He's too scared to buy them himself, in case it ruins his reputation."

"What reputation?"

"Well, exactly. Still, I get to keep the change and since he gives me a day or two I always get to read them first. Sometimes, if they're up to scratch, I even swipe the centrefolds. I keep them in the glove compartment."

33

Glove compartment. Righty-ho.

"So, he reads them in the office, when there's no-one else around?"

"Right. Mostly afternoons, while Mary's working in the shop. He reads the adverts too, y'know, he's always sending off for stuff. Once, I saw an order for a jar of 'Big Boy Stallion Cream'!"

We laughed so hard the whole van shook. Then he left with a bundle of mail. He came back clutching a brown paper bag. Dog biscuits. Kenny was *good*.

Next it was a shabby old farm which I remembered from my youth. There was a sheepdog chained to a fence but otherwise it looked deserted. Kenny got out and looked around then walked across to a big wooden gate and stuffed some mail in a piece of piping wedged between the upper slats. The dog leapt up and made a commotion. Kenny didn't seem concerned. He scanned the area once again before clambering back in the van.

"Nothing on offer out here?" I asked.

"Plenty," he said, "but not just now. Last weekend I flattened his dog. That one there's a new recruit."

"He's upset?"

"Not with me, he didn't *see* me do it, but if *he'd* been out and about today, the new dog would have got a biscuit."

Right, I was catching on. Things were suddenly making sense. Towards the end of that lazy morning the van was full of fresh farm produce *and* I knew which farmers' wives were worth a glimpse in their undergarments. None of them appealed to me but Kenny's tastes were quite unique, he'd fantasise about all of them and some were practically pensioners. He'd pointed out his current favourite, Rosie Roberts was her name, a lovely lady, yes, I'm sure, but she was built for pulling carts.

"But what about those *tits?*" Kenny squealed.

"What about them?" I suggested. "Larger ones, from *my* experience, don't respond to stimulation."

"Please," he groaned, "you're not suggesting anorexic types are better? Skin and bone's a turn-off, man! Where's your sense of adventure, eh? You need a woman with plenty to grapple with, think about it, fat's erotic! Huge, opulent mounds of flesh!"

Well, I thought. Each to their own.

The last call was to Green Hills Farm which overlooked the sewage works. A single letter remained in the basket, posted second class.

Kenny held it up to the light.

"D'ya reckon we should risk it?"

"How the hell should *I* know?" I snapped. "What in God's name are we dealing with?"

"Hmm, well, it *could* be important . . ."

"Look," I said, "stop messing about! You're supposed to be *training* me, let's get the bloody thing delivered!"

So, we drove along a track and ended up in a quaint little farmyard. There was a rockery, flowers galore and an ornamental fishpond.

"Lock the door," Kenny demanded.

I locked mine, he locked his. Then he gave a blast on the horn which caught me just a little off guard.

"Jesus Christ! *KENNY!*" I yelled.

He acted very nonchalant. He slowly slid down into his seat and slightly adjusted the brim of his cap.

I wasn't quite sure what to think. There was silence, for a moment, then a sudden hail of thudding, coming from the back of the van. *Thump-a thump-a thump-thump-thump!!!* "What the fuck was that?" I gasped. It sounded like we were under siege, being peppered with bullets, here, in Trimley! I was almost on the floor. What the hell was going on? My first thought was a robbery but we had nothing left to rob! What had Kenny been doing up here? Murder? Rape? It didn't seem fair. This had nothing to do with me, yet here I was, trapped in a van with possibly only seconds to live! *BANG-A BANG-A BANG-BANG-BANG!!!* The noise was getting progressively louder, the van was rocking from side to side from whatever it was that was slamming into us. Meanwhile Kenny simply sat there, I was missing something here, then gradually as the shock wore off and my brain began to focus a little, I filtered out some unusual sounds, in amongst the noise and confusion. Hollow, nasal, vaguely familiar, almost a screech but duller than that. I plucked up the courage to check the wing mirror . . . what was that in the air . . . *feathers?*

Finally, the penny dropped: "Geese! Shit! Killer geese!" Though I felt a tad relieved they seemed to be surrounding us.

At last, Kenny opened his mouth: "There's dogs an' all and those are worse! Rottweilers! Enormous things! Once, they ripped me mudflaps off!"

"Did they ever meet our Jack?"

"Nah. Never got the chance. One time was enough for him. Ben was roped in after that."

Meanwhile the assault went on, the geese kept pounding and pounding away, then just as I was beginning to think they'd have to send for a rescue crew, a burly bloke with his shirt undone came marching across from the farmhouse door. He winked at us then spat on the ground as Kenny carefully opened the window, sliding him the solitary letter through what was barely a quarter-inch gap. We watched him with anticipation, shirt-tails flapping about in the breeze. He scanned the envelope, ripped it up, then fed the pieces to the geese.

"Rats!" said Kenny. "Thought as much!"

It had been a waste of time. Nevertheless I was there to learn and now I was aware of the dangers: ghastly geese, deadly dogs, fearsome farmers with woeful wives. Kenny had a second wage but really had to work for it.

"So," I asked, "we're finally done?"

"Yup," he sighed, "the show's over."

"What a ride!"

"Thought you'd like it. Same again tomorrow?"

"Aye."

There were other duties like the parcel run and the box collections, they were done in the afternoons, but hardly required any special training. Still, it did mean overtime since you were out for most of the day. Sadly, I was second cover. That meant rarely needed.

8

The drinks meanwhile did not relent. Some of my hangovers were spectacular. Why I never phoned in sick, I'm not too sure, stupidity? Although I'd made a promise to Ed and thus my honour was at stake, no-one ever phoned in sick. It simply wasn't done.

But some days it was hard to take. One day *very* hard. After umpteen pints and little sleep I somehow got to work on time and stumbled into the office glare deplete of all resources. I slumped down onto my rickety stool. Ed and Jack were not impressed. I sat there like a tender sapling, swaying in the breeze . . .

Sleep, sleep, sleep, sleep . . . every cell demanded it . . . finally I'd had enough, and since we had a sorting table, sat right there in front of me, I clambered onto it, clumsily, as everybody else looked on, then turned and stretched out onto my back and pulled a mail sack over my face.

The suit was there to greet me when I stumbled in the following day. He wasn't there to sing my praises. Jack's face told the story.

I was led away for privacy.

"Still no uniform, Mr Peagerm?"

"No, not yet, there's always Christmas."

That went down like a lead balloon.

"Eric," he said with a weary sigh, "look, I'll get to the point, OK? You've been reported drunk on duty. What have you got to say for yourself?"

"*Drunk?*" I asked, hamming it up.

"Yes. Drunk. Intoxicated."

"Under the weather, possibly, yes. Too many nights on the town, perhaps. But drunk? *Me?* Certainly not! Who's been telling you this?"

"Your boss."

"Look, we have to get up at five. Can't we have a social life?"

"Yes, of course, nevertheless we must conform to certain standards. We provide a service and we have responsibilities, and ours, as you very well know, is to Royal Mail and to all of its customers. Presentation is paramount, so if they see you rolling drunk, it tarnishes the image we have, a clever lad like you should *see* that."

"Yes, of course, but I wasn't drunk!" (I wasn't all that clever either). "I was tucked up in bed by midnight, what the hell do you want me to do? Pick up the phone and call in sick, whenever I'm a little groggy? No-one else in here does that and I *refuse* to be the first. I'm always in, eventually, no matter *how* unwell I'm feeling. Doesn't that count for anything here? Doesn't it show that I'm *committed?* Anyway, while we're at it, how did *he* know I was drunk?"

"He used to run a Public House. He *should* know what a drunk looks like."

"No! Not at six in the morning! Not unless he flaunted the law! Drunk at the end of a bar's one thing but a lack of sleep's entirely another!"

"Look," he said, "I know for a fact you can easily do this job half drunk. Any fool can . . ."

"And some do."

"Yes, but as I said, we all have standards. Therefore this is a verbal warning. From tomorrow, when you arrive, make sure you're in a reasonable state, if not you'll be sent back home and you'll be suspended without hesitation. Think about your future, Eric. Think about your livelihood. One more warning then you're out. No-one's indispensable."

And that was that, my card was marked. It was Ben all over again. I thought about him teaching kids . . . *hmmm, better him than me*. But how much did I want this job? Was it really worth the fuss? My options seemed a little stark, sobriety or back to the dole. I didn't fancy either of those, not much fun or not much cash. What the hell, I couldn't decide. I'd have to tough it out a while.

The mail was in by that point so I went outside to help unload it. "What's *he* want in there?" asked Dave, our sixteen-stone delivery driver.

"My arse on a stick," I said, "but guess what, he can kiss it first!"

"Good lad, he's a slimy get, but stand your ground and you'll be fine."

By noon I'd made a compromise, another shopping list solution. Vitamins and liver salts and the strongest coffee that money could buy. Plus, I reset my alarm to revive me a whole ten minutes earlier. Sacrificing my beauty sleep. The things you had to do for a job!

9

I found that liver salts gave you the wind, or more wind if you already had it. Saturday mornings were bad enough but soon they became unbearable. With Kenny's belly full of beans and mine and Tony's full of ale, the atmosphere inside the office could only be described as *rancid*. Jack meanwhile had a simple defence: once infected air was detected he'd purse his lips and whistle a tune, a clever little strategy to blow the stench away from his face. Kenny and I discussed this and decided that, from that point on, whenever either of *us* let fly we'd also whistle a merry tune; not just as a piss-take but as an early warning system too, a signal of the forthcoming odour steadily clawing its way through the air. Sheila shunned the whole idea but Tony and Harry were quickly on board and thus between the four of us a whole new office procedure was born: whenever someone blew a fart, a jaunty whistle-off would start. First the guilty one, then Jack. The tunes themselves were variable. Our Ed would make the occasional comment: "You'd think we had canaries in here!" Canaries would have stood *no* chance. The mines had been less dangerous.

Otherwise it was business as usual, Jack was never quiet for long. If the farting wasn't an issue the size of his walk would set him away. Now and then a local firm would buy some land and build some houses and if they built them on *his* walk he'd moan about it continually.

"*More* bloody houses? Come on, Ed! Mine's the only walk that's growing! The best I can do for a break these days is rush down a can of pop and a biscuit!"

That of course was ridiculous, he never did *anything* in a rush; although his walk was slightly expanding he still got home an hour early and claimed his overtime like the rest of us. What the hell was he moaning for? Some folks had to work hard for a living. His constant griping was getting us down. He was like a permanent itch.

Ed grew sick of his whining too. "What am *I* supposed to do?"

"Take some bloody pressure off me! *You're* supposed to be the boss! Why not redesign the walks? All I'm asking for is fairness! Eric's got the lightest walk! *He* can take a few of *my* streets!"

That was hardly practical, his walk was miles away from mine, but even if it hadn't been, I wasn't taking streets from *him*. *I* suggested rotating the walks, where Sheila, Tony, Jack and myself would do a different walk each week, so things would even out each month. Of course, I knew what Jack would say, his house was on his current walk. He liked to have his tea break with his feet up at the kitchen table.

"No!" he squealed. "Not a chance, we shouldn't have to change our walks! That would make things three times harder, I want something *easier!*"

"Euthanasia?" I suggested.

"Ed! Ed! Did you hear *that?* One more crack from *you* my lad and I'm on the phone to Regional Office!"

Ed however got there first and asked a suit to sort it out, but he was reluctant to get involved, encouraging *us* to find a solution as *we* were the ones with the local knowledge. And he was right, for once in his life, so that put everything back to square one and it all went round and round in circles, me and Jack having slanging matches and everyone else avoiding the issue. Which grew tiresome after a while and Kenny was the first to crack, offering to relieve Jack of a handful of his more 'awkward' deliveries. Schools, Doctors, that sort of thing, which took around twenty minutes on foot, the van meanwhile could do them in ten, except there was a little catch: Kenny's offer was on condition that *I'd* assist with the afternoon parcels. That one stopped me in my tracks. What did it have to do with *me?* Ed appeared to like the idea and though Jack wasn't *too* impressed, he did concede it was better than nothing, which, for him, seemed *very* gracious. I was having none of it though, to me it sounded like surrender, why should *I* work extra while the rest got overtime for nothing? Still, I said I'd give it some thought. Maybe I was missing something? Kenny knew much more than I and this had all been *his* idea.

Later, it was clarified. Kenny sought me out with the van. He pulled up with a bacon sandwich, fresh from one of the farmhouse kitchens. "Listen, Eric," he said between mouthfuls, "I've had quite enough of Jack. We need to shut him up somehow or else I'll end up throttlin' him!"

"Fine," I said, "I understand, but what's it got to do with me? Twenty minutes off *his* shift in exchange for shafting *me* with sixty? What the hell do *I* get out of it?"

"Van experience."

"Great. What else?"

"Doesn't it take you half an hour to walk back home from work each day?"

"Aye?"

"Well, I'll drop you off. On your doorstep, with the van. That'll save you half an hour."

"What about the other half?"

"What about it? That's not much, considering all the *overtime*. No-one counts the parcels Eric, not even me, at least not properly. Ed's not bothered, as you know, and twelve or more means overtime, so if I say there's twenty-four, then twenty-four there is!"

"Oh."

And delivering parcels wasn't so bad, at least it didn't involve the farms, the housing estates had one or two hazards but nothing like the countryside. We drove around at a reasonable pace, there wasn't a schedule to adhere to, Ed didn't care what time we returned, as long as we did, eventually.

We kept the parcels behind the seats, the back of the van was for business only. Kenny would trade throughout the day so the van was always full of his crap.

"How much do you make from this?"

"Not much cash, it's mostly bartering."

"What's your motivation then?"

"Helps to pass the time, I guess."

I told him if he used *my* time he'd have to give me a share of the profits. "How about twenty-five per cent?"

"How about *zero*, cheeky get!"

But there we were in the van each day, overtime could not have been easier. There was our 'virtual' overtime but that was more of a bonus payment. This was work we almost did and it was a breeze compared to the walks. Kenny did the driving while I sat and barked out all the addresses.

Amongst his other peculiarities, Kenny was intrigued by parcels. He would hold them up in the air and give them a little squeeze or a shake. "Whaddya think of this one?" he'd ask. "Animal, vegetable, or the other?"

"What's the other?"

"Battery powered."

I didn't care, I just wanted rid of them.

And we made good use of our time, I'd leap from the van to deliver a parcel and if the next address was close then Kenny would rattle off down the road and meet me halfway coming back.

We pulled up at a house in Colton across the road from The Old White Horse. The front door (mostly frosted glass) had a huge behind pressed up against it.

"I suppose that this one's yours?"

"No."

"Why?"

"No bare flesh."

Kenny had specific tastes. We were very different people. Yet he sat and watched me as I trotted up the garden path. Maybe she was mental or she had a vicious dog or something? Either way, I rapped on the door while she went up and down with a hoover. I was rapping pretty hard but the roar appeared to be drowning me out. I rapped and rapped to no avail so I dropped to my knees and yelled through the letterbox: "PARCEL! PARCEL! MRS WATTS? COME AND GET IT WHILE IT'S WRAPPED!"

No response.

"*OOOOOYYYYY!!!!!*" I screamed.

That appeared to do the trick. She stopped and turned the racket off and shouted out instructions:

"*SHOVE IT IN ME PASSAGE, WILL YA?*"

"WHAT ABOUT THE PARCEL, PET?"

The next one rattled like broken glass.

We left it for another day.

10

Then, after sixteen months, my Royal Mail uniform finally arrived. There it was on my bench one morning, a slipshod stack of polythene parcels. Four cotton shirts, all sky blue, a couple of pairs of sturdy trousers, one peaked cap, a sweater, a tie, a jacket, a coat and a set of waterproofs. All apart from the shirts were navy, tastefully edged with bright red piping. Shoes were not supplied back then, the damn things wore out *far* too fast.

The waterproofs were a waste of time, resisting the rain but retaining your body heat, thus you teemed with rivers of sweat and ended up soaking wet regardless. But the tie could save your life, a clip-on affair, which suited me fine. Mornings were a chore at best, I doubt I could have coped with knots. The idea was that should you be mugged and grabbed by the tie, as all muggers do, the thing would just snap off in their hand, which gave you a chance to make your escape. A great idea, clean and simple, no need for alarms or sprays, I had the ultimate protection, a new Royal Mail security tie! I wondered if there were vacancies for bright young uniform designers, that seemed like the easy life, all ideas and not much sweat. They could have locked me in a room with a bunch of creative art school types and I could have sat around all day being utterly pretentious.

But there I was after sixteen months, a man who finally looked the part. It gave me an air of responsibility, people in the street would say so.

"Look at Eric, doesn't he look *dignified?*"

"Oooh, aye, he scrubs up well!"

"No, it *can't* be, wait, it *is!*"

This went on for months on end.

I didn't enjoy conforming to standards but understood the power of the uniform. *I* didn't care how anyone dressed but the general public surely did. They liked to have us looking smart, a uniform would put them at ease, they'd all been brainwashed to believe that a uniform meant impeccable character. I was officially Royal Mail now and my brand new outfit commanded respect. Old ladies would realise I wasn't a student. Younger ones would beam me a smile. And dozens of kids on their way to school could point and jeer and sing in unison:

"POSTMAN PAT, POSTMAN PAT, POSTMAN PAT AND HIS BLACK AND WHITE CAAAAAAAAAAT!!!"

Oh joy.

Then all of a sudden a body clock hit me. How and why was a mystery. It woke me up at five in the morning, seconds before the alarm was due. At first I thought I had psychic powers, my brain was in tune with the clock-spring tension. Then they told me it was normal. That was such a disappointment.

"Why's it only just kicked in?"

"Alcoholic delay," they said. "If you hadn't been a drinker, this would have happened a year ago."

It could have been a blessing if it hadn't applied to Sundays too. Plus, it switched me off at ten. Fine if I was back at home and slumped in front of the TV screen, but dangerous if I was out there, perched on top of a rickety barstool. One pub had an open fire and there I was known as 'The Phoenix of Trimley'. Liz, the owner, gave me the name, a sultry type with long black hair and the tightest jeans you could ever wish for. I'd start nodding off at ten. I was helpless to prevent it. Fortunately Liz would be watching and she would rush from the bar to my rescue whenever I'd lean towards the flames. None of my mates would assist, of course, they found the whole thing quite hilarious. I'd be mostly none the wiser, except one time when Liz was delayed by a minor fracas at the bar and she ended up grabbing me harder than usual, plunging her fingernails into my nipples. That revived me well enough. Pain and pleasure, rolled into one.

"Liz," I moaned, "you really care!"

"I care about my friggin' licence!"

Then, at the Legion club, they locked me in one Saturday night. I'd dozed off in a secluded corner and woke up all alone in the dark. Though I realised where I was, the shutters at the bar were down and I was forced to escape through a fire door, thus setting off the burglar alarm. It was one of those wailing sirens, naturally I ran away, but the following day, word got out that there'd been a break-in during the night. Apparently, the fag machine, some speakers and the TV were missing. Insurance fraud or burglary? Either way, my mouth stayed shut.

Consequently my spirits were low, this body clock business was a nuisance. I was now in serious danger of making an utter fool of myself. I toyed with possible solutions, I took naps in the afternoons, but that only gave me sleep paralysis, an unnerving state of affairs where your brain wakes up before your body does, leaving you with eyes wide open but otherwise unable to move. Next I tried having less to drink, but that had no effect on it either, as soon as ten o'clock approached . . . *slump* . . . I was out for the count. It got to the stage where *everyone* knew, often they'd be sat in wait, I dropped off in The Ox one night and woke up with an eyebrow missing. That one finished me off for good, I'd made myself a laughing stock. From then on ten o'clock meant bedtime, there was simply no way round it. Not that any of this should have mattered, licensing laws were strict back then. Come eleven the night should have ended but often it had barely begun. Most of the pubs had stoppy-backs with scant regard for the licensing laws. Little chance of a raid, y'see. Coppers were the *last* to leave.

11

My walk meanwhile had one advantage, most of it was council houses. Everything was open plan, therefore instead of using the paths I'd simply cut across the lawns in a beeline for the next address. I saved a lot of time this way, although there was a price to pay, the lawns were always soaking wet with morning dew or the constant drizzle. Thus my feet were always wet. Wellies were the obvious answer. They would slow you down somewhat but dryer feet could mean less colds. I always seemed to have one so I mentioned it to Kenny one day, who promised me a quality pair, as long as I promised to slip him a fiver. They would cost him less, of course, and quality meant something else to him, but they were twice as much in the shops and so I took him up on the offer.

"No steel toecaps, mind you," I said, "they have to be light enough for walking. And remember I take size 12, not 11 or 13 or anything else!"

Naturally I feared the worst, I knew him well enough by now, he'd find a pair of size 10 steelies and rip out the steel to make more room. Well, OK, whatever, I thought, a fiver wouldn't break me, if they helped to keep my feet dry then I didn't need perfection.

He dumped them on my bench next morning, they looked pretty good to me. I tried them on and they fit quite well so I gladly handed him the cash.

"That reminds me," he began, "did I ever tell you Ben's old story?"

"Which one's that?"

"The wellies one."

"No. Never."

And off he went.

Ben had been driving his car through the rain, one of Kenny's old patchwork affairs, and he'd came across a bit of a flood on the old back road from Statton to Trimley. As he'd tried to tackle it the water gushed in through the floor, and since he had his sandals on, his feet got well and truly soaked. At least his wellies were in the boot, it always pays to be prepared, but when he'd tried to slip them on, he'd found he'd packed his six-year-old son's!

Kenny had more stories than Ed but at least his tales were entertaining, unlike Ed's they had a point and he didn't repeat them over and over. There was one from his early teens, he'd meet his mates behind the pit-heap and since they'd all reached puberty they'd have these masturbation contests. They would gather round in a circle and throw a penny each in the pot, then they'd get their peckers out and the first to reach a climax won. Try to picture it in your mind, half a dozen scruffy young tykes, thrashing away for all they were worth with sweaty brows, flushed faces and spittle steaming from their palms. Finally one would give out a groan and ejaculate, triumphantly, before legging it down the road with the cash, tucking his shirt tails in on the way. The rest of the gang would be left behind, panting away in desperation, either on the vinegar strokes or having been forced to accept defeat. You weren't allowed to cheat either. Saucy pictures of Diana Dors (or whoever they lusted after back then) were strictly against the rules of the game, inspiration had to be imagined. Not that Kenny would have such thoughts, he claimed to be naive back then. All he had on his mind was the cash, which might explain why he never won.

But enough of that, back to the wellies. They were quickly broken in. They'd already passed the waterproof test and soon enough they were tested for strength. One misty morning I was approached by a scruffy old man on Redstone Road, accompanied by a flea-bitten mutt on the end of what looked like

50

a home-made lead. The pair of them were quite a sight, the guy was like a decrepit scarecrow, the dog however looked ten times worse with a greasy, grey-brown, matted coat and sunken eyes, much darker and hollow, surrounded by a sticky film that appeared to be forming a solid crust. The poor old thing was wasting away, it looked like it was harmless enough, but just as they were passing me by, with me attempting to look indifferent, it suddenly made a lunge for my leg, the left one, just below the knee. Luckily its teeth found rubber, I was glad to have those wellies, nevertheless it gripped me tight and the damn thing wasn't about to let go. The scarecrow stood there in a trance. "Get this bloody thing off!" I demanded. He was either deaf or daft. "Come on, don't just stand there, *pull!*"

Finally, he tugged at the lead.

"Harder," I yelled, "give it some welly!"

"It's got some!"

"Oh, you think that's *funny?* Get this fucking thing off me, NOW, before I do summat we'll BOTH regret!"

He pulled one way, I pulled the other. The dog held firm, clamped to my leg. The tug-of-war went on and on, it must have looked ridiculous. It just required a bit of thought. What would Kenny do, I wondered? He'd have biscuits in his pockets. I had paracetamol. I thought of sliding out of the welly but that would have left my leg exposed. Then I thought of mind games, *yes!* Surely I could defeat a dog? I quickly dropped down onto one knee and I gave the hound a steely glare. It growled and glared right back at me. It clearly didn't want to play. I was running out of options, not to mention patience, so I snatched the lead from its so-called master, grabbed a hold of the dog's rear end, then dragged it steadily within range and gave it a hefty boot up the arse. To my dismay it didn't work, the dog gave out a muffled yelp, but kept a solid grip on my leg, a firmer grip, if anything. His owner was a waste of space. "Come on, Jasper, let him go!" Which, of course, had no effect, and thus I slid my pouches off and grabbed the beast by the root of its tail, then reached around where no man should and gave its plums an admonishing squeeze.

At last it released me, yelping and whining.

"Hey! Hey! There was no need for that!"

"No?" I snarled, annoyed to the max. "What else was I supposed to do? Stand there like a fucking *goon* till one of us finally died of old age?"

"Well . . ."

"No! Keep it shut! And keep that bloody thing off the streets! And while you're at it, give it a feed, then get it sorted out at the vet's!"

I knew it was a waste of breath, a nation of animal lovers indeed. But I couldn't help thinking, out of the three of us, just who needed training the most?

Though dogs were not a major problem, every now and then there were incidents. I was a postman after all. We weren't supposed to get along. The Royal Mail set up Parcelforce, an early attempt at privatisation, which destroyed the afternoon run and hit us pretty hard in the pocket. The new 'force' took control of the parcels and though we had a few large packets, even doubling the number of those would rarely earn us any overtime. Soon I was doing the packets alone while Kenny despatched a few in the mornings. This not only cost me cash, but also half an hour each day as when I dropped the van keys off I had to make my own way home. Despite these new annoyances, Mrs Mead got packets daily, she lived down in Grangeworth Road and a young Jack Russell patrolled her garden. I would honk the horn at her gate and out she'd come in her overalls, and then, with all arms stretched in the air, I'd carefully try to pass her the packet while Fido leapt up and down like a maniac, trying his best to intercept it. *Boing! Boing! Boing!* he would go, like he was on a trampoline, snarling and snapping away with his teeth but just not quite achieving his goal. Until, one day, with all that practice his legs had strengthened up to the point where, with a good six-foot leap in the air, he finally managed to match my reach and snatch the packet away from my grasp. Mrs Mead just stood there, stunned, it *had* been quite a considerable feat, though I was more concerned with the red stuff, spurting from my fingertips. Although I got a week on the sick I couldn't stop my fingers throbbing. Day and night, my right hand too, and that, my friend, made *everything* difficult.

Yet the worst was still to come, the Savage Pit Bull of Parkdale Road. They hadn't banned the breed back then and every numbskull seemed to have one. It would stand at the window each morning, watching, waiting, *simmering* with hatred, perched precariously on the ledge, its ears and tail erect and alert, its murderous yellow eyes on fire. The thing would *erupt* whenever it saw me. Had we met in a previous life? I knew that dogs were territorial, still, it did feel *personal*. As I approached the window each day, the pane would be awash with saliva and as I quickly scurried past, its teeth would hammer against the glass as the beast achieved new heights of insanity. Then, one day, the ledge was empty, everything was strangely still, but all the same I felt uneasy and, sure enough, as I passed the house, a rather squalid-looking semi, I caught a glimpse of the crazy animal, stomping around in the yard at the back. At once it seemed to sense my presence and suddenly whipped up into a frenzy and though I wasn't *too* concerned, no way could it have jumped the fence, so fierce was its determination it heaved its oversized head against it, straining the slats with each new attempt, every so often using its skull as a primitive kind of battering ram. I must have been fifty yards away when I heard the sound of splintering wood, followed by a much louder *CRACK!* and I spun around, filled with dread, only to find my fears confirmed, the hound had managed to smash its way through and was hurtling in a bee-line towards me. *Shit, this is it,* I thought, *too late to run and nowhere to hide!* All I had was instinct, so I yanked my pouches off my back and held them out in front of me, as sixty-odd pounds of muscle and teeth came speeding at me like a torpedo. No more Sunday League for me, or maybe any future sex life? Either way, I knew for sure that this was going to *really hurt.* And yet, somehow, it didn't happen.

Well, not to me at least. The Fates were on my side that day though, God knows why, I hardly deserved it. As the beast was closing in, a smaller dog appeared on the scene, a jaunty little mongrel that I'd often seen around that way. And the pit bull went for that, darting to its right in an instant, smashing into it, sideways on, before clamping its huge jaws onto its neck with a cruel and frightening precision. There was no time to react, for me *or* the poor little dog. I shuddered and stood there, mortified, as the pit bull throttled its lifeless quarry.

Other streets were notable too, but for very different reasons. Daley Road was one example, nightwear was the theme along there. No.6 was gorgeous, she had umpteen kids but I envied her husband. It was a joy when she came to the door for a package too large to squeeze through her letterbox. Most of the time they weren't too large but it didn't stop me knocking her up. I must have done it twice a week when once a fortnight would have sufficed. She'd stand there in a towelling robe which scarcely concealed the assets she had, those breasts, those hips, that body seemed *ripe*, as if it were *bursting* to escape. No such luck at No.12, I didn't want *her* to burst out of anything, she was built like a Sherman tank and would stand there every single morning, stood on the step with a scowl on her face, an undersized cardigan over her nightgown, stretched to the limit by boundless flesh. If I was stood at No.6 she'd stand there blocking the light from her doorway, huge arms folded whatever the weather, glaring with intense disapproval, blazing eyes demanding the mail. But often there was worse to come, the other end of the street was *scary*, her in No.66 was one 6 short of a biblical prophecy. Any inner beauty had been deeply swathed in something else, the first time being by far the worst, being unprepared for any of it. I stood there in the pouring rain, rapping at the door, unwell. I had a County Court demand and had to get a signature. At last, there were signs of life, I heard her tramping down the stairs, but when she finally opened up I was hit in the face by a terrible smell. It was the smell of sweat and dirt, an overpowering stench of neglect, accumulated over time through a wanton lack of any hygiene. Sadly it was not unusual, most walks had a hovel or two, but this one was exceptional and I felt the bile hit the back of my throat. Then I saw who'd opened the door, it certainly wasn't for the timid, my instincts told me to look away, but somehow I was mesmerised. I saw the greasy greying hair, glued to her brow with a film of sweat, I saw the battered old NHS glasses with grimy lenses half an inch thick, I saw the terrible skin condition, worse than *I'd* had during my teens, which gave her flesh a mottled effect, the remainder deeply pitted with dirt. Her swollen belly was barely contained by the ragged old nightie hung from her shoulders, way too small and torn at the seams, and though one time it may have been white it was now ingrained with a putrid old mess, with egg and ketchup and gravy on there, or chocolate perhaps, there was no way of telling. I shuddered to think what else was involved, the woman was gross beyond comprehension. "Sorry," I said as I bowed my head and vomited onto her doorstep.

12

Mostly I was single, I was rubbish with the ladies, but I didn't mind being on my own, at least it kept things fairly simple. I got up, went off to work, came home, played music, masturbated, watched TV, went down the pub and played a bit of Sunday football. That was it, it wasn't hard, a stress-free life was all you needed. Boyfriends, girlfriends, husbands and wives just complicated everything. I'd had a girlfriend in my teens which lasted for a year or so, but that had ended so miserably that I'd lost all faith in romantic relationships. Human beings were selfish and found compromise quite taxing, so unless you were a perfect match I failed to see how things could work. I studied couples, watched their behaviour, some had two distinct personalities, one for when their partners were there and another one for when they weren't. Was it simply instinct or a conscious game of strategy? Either way, I didn't care, it all seemed like an elaborate con.

Then, one morning, I was out being lashed by a storm of extreme persistence, trying to force the rain-soaked mail through unforgiving letterboxes. Most of it was falling apart, such filthy weather showed no mercy, some complained but I laughed it off, they'd have to take it up with Ed. Despite all this I soldiered on, until I found an open doorway, Bob and Jean O'Reilly's house, I'd often see them in the boozer. Even though they had no mail I felt compelled to look inside. Kenny said that open doors were golden opportunities.

So I looked and there was Jean, beyond the hallway in the kitchen. It looked warm and dry in there. I was cold and very wet.

A mental picture quickly formed, my bare feet on the kitchen table, socks across the radiator, kettle on the boil.

"This carpet's getting damp down here!"

"Not as damp as *you*, I'll bet!"

Jean had spun around to face me, coffee cup in hand.

Right.

"Oh, I bet that coffee's good!"

"Alright Eric, come on in."

"*Sanctuary*," I muttered as I hurried through the door.

Jean was in her early forties, lightly tanned with long blonde hair. Bob meanwhile was almost sixty. Bob had rode his luck, it seemed. Jean was always smartly dressed and had an easy going manner. Didn't seem to have a job. Occasionally, things made sense.

I let my pouches fall to the floor and struggled from my overcoat. I slung it on the hallway rack which almost buckled under the weight.

Another coffee cup appeared as I parked myself at the kitchen table.

"How do you like it?"

"What?"

"Your coffee!"

"Oh! White and sweet please, Jean."

We sat there at the table, chatting. Bob had gone to work, you know. We mostly talked about the rain but all the while she seemed flirtatious. I was mystified by this. I was tall but not so handsome. Something didn't quite add up. Perhaps I was imagining it? Then she suddenly reached towards me and took a sleeve of my shirt in her hand, and kneading it between her fingers, whispered, "*Eric, your shirt's all wet.*"

"Dry me off then," I suggested, praying I hadn't misread the signs. She took another sip from her cup while I just sat there like a tripod.

"Right, I'll get a towel then."

I followed her rear end up the stairs.

"How long have we got?" she asked.

"Long enough."

The job could wait.

I scrambled out of the rest of my clothes while Jean was closing the bedroom curtains, then I vaulted over the bed and spun her around to face me. She barely had the time to gasp as I firmly planted my lips onto hers, then dragged her hips in tight to mine which almost lifted her clear from the floor. Whatever clothing she had on came off with scant regard for the fabric. There she was, completely naked. *Jean, oh Jean,* I thought to myself, *you've just restored my faith in humanity!* We fell backwards onto the bed as our lips and tongues got reacquainted, my hands exploring every inch of that curvy miracle of a body. Then she suddenly grabbed my cock and guided it between her thighs. I struggled to retain control . . . it had been a long, long time. I'd feared that if she touched it I'd have shot my wad all over the sheets, but somehow I was still in the game, so I swiftly spun her onto her back and then gently eased myself inside her. What a feeling of joy *that* was, locked in the grip of eternal glory, now I just had to keep it there, so I tried to keep it slow at first, those first-time fucks were clumsy affairs, but it rarely worked and before too long we were banging away like a couple of monkeys incapable of rational thought. Everything in the room was shaking, bedposts were slamming against the wall, floorboards were creaking, nightstands rattling, both of us were drenched in sweat.

Then, suddenly, it was over. I dismounted and stared at the ceiling. Jean leapt up and made for the bathroom. Neither one of us were smokers. Meanwhile I was still at work so I grabbed my clothes and returned downstairs. I cleaned up at the kitchen sink then sat back down in my underwear.

I sat there for a minute or two. My coffee cup was still quite warm. Shortly after Jean came down, flushed but fully dressed again. She smiled and put the kettle on then opened up the morning paper. I was at a loss for words. What was I supposed to say?

Finally I broke the silence.

"So . . . what about safe sex?"

"*What?*"

"Well, y'know, *safe sex*. Condoms, the pill . . . *that* sort of thing."

"What about it?"

"Don't you use them?"

"Not any more. What about *you?*"

"Well, yes, it does make sense but I never thought I'd need them at work!"

I asked her if she had any kids. No, ovarian cancer, see, which killed that line of conversation and forced me into getting dressed.

I sat back down, uncomfortably. My clothes were still quite cold and damp. The streets meanwhile were out there waiting. Then she finally let me have it.

"Listen," she told me, "this is important. I'll be getting a registered letter. When it arrives, promise me, you won't come knocking till after eight."

"Will it be addressed to *you?*"

"Yes."

"Alright then, not a problem."

"Promise?"

"Promise."

"When do we knock?"

"Chocolate mints. After eight."

And soon enough the letter arrived. From the County Court, no less. God knows what the hell she'd done but it was nothing to do with me. I kept my word accordingly and knocked her up at ten-past eight. She signed for it with a look of relief, then slammed the door in my face.

13

Winter was coming. So were the '90s. It was getting cold and dark. Suddenly I was feeling it, as now my body clock ruled my life I couldn't drink as much as I used to and consequently my nervous system was more aware of the plummeting temperatures. Darkness had its downside too, especially where there were no street lights, those winding roads from Trimley to Statton were deadly at the best of times. I thought a little car might help, I had some money in the bank, and if I had to blow the lot I could always pay the insurance monthly. Then I thought about the extras: petrol, road tax, MOT, replacement tyres, brake fluid, oil, repairs if I should have a crash, the list appeared to be never-ending. When I totalled everything up and related it to the cost of beer, it seemed that, on the balance of things, a car was hardly worth it.

It proved to be a bad decision. That particular winter was fierce. Snow hit hard in early December and hung around for months on end. Snow was a nightmare for a postie, heavy snow especially, as tramping through it wore you down and at any given moment in time a sudden roof-fall could bury you alive. And the children didn't help. Kids were evil in the snow. When there wasn't snow on the ground, 'Postman Pat' was all they could muster but when there was, between renditions, they'd pepper me with snowballs too. Every school day, always the same . . . *splat!* . . . one on the back of my neck, cold snow dripping down my spine . . . *splat!* . . . one on the back of my leg, wet snow sliding into my wellies . . . *splat!* . . . one on the side of my head, almost knocking my cap clean off . . . and should I *dare*

60

to turn and face them . . . *splat!* . . . I'd get one square in the face. I could hardly retaliate, I rarely saw the guilty party and even if I did, what then? Beating up a nine-year-old is frowned upon in Public Service. So, I'd give them an evil stare, as if to memorise their faces, one day they'd be all grown up and *then* we'd see how clever they were. I'd done similar things, of course, but I'd been squarely punished when caught. Nowadays it wasn't allowed. Should you lay a hand on them at the very least you'd lose your job and if the parents were so inclined they just might cart you off to jail.

The snow made everything a chore, the walk to work took twice as long, the Statton road was flanked by fields and snow would drift at every corner. It was just as bad on the streets, people rarely cleared the footpaths. It would slow me down so much I'd hardly ever get back on time. Not unless I caught a bus and the 10:45 was the cut-off point. Miss that and it was all too late, the outgoing mail would miss the collection. Still, when the weather was good the buses were unpredictable. When it snowed they couldn't cope. You simply had to take pot luck.

One morning, I'd completed my walk and already emptied two of my boxes. One remained, outside the shops. My watch was reading 10:42. I found my keys and opened it up, to find the whole thing chock-full of snow. Not a huge surprise, in truth, occasionally there'd be cigarette butts and often the contents would go up in smoke. Sometimes there'd be a corpse in there, a bird perhaps, or maybe a mouse. If you were lucky, a nice dog turd. How the children like to play! Still, I had a job to do so I started filling a pouch with snow. There was a letter or two in there but I couldn't be arsed with separation. I was interrupted, of course, to be told the thing had been blocked all morning, so I still had plenty to do when the bus came rolling into view. Wheel-deep snow yet bang on time, or an hour late, you couldn't tell. Such things hardly mattered when you simply wanted to get on board. Either way, I had to decide, whether to leave the box as it was and jump on the bus with what I had, or to stay and finish the box and therefore miss the outward collection. Tough call but I plumped for the latter. The mail would get there eventually. Ed was sure to give me grief but that was nothing new. So, I cleared the box and locked it up then headed off towards the shops. The next bus was the 10:59. Plenty time for sustenance. I bought myself a hot cheese slice and ate it up against a wall, pondering the universe while keeping an eye out for the bus. A little old lady grabbed my arm. "I need to post this birthday card! Would you hang on there a bit, until I get a first-class stamp?" She'd bolted into the paper shop before I had a chance to answer, barging to the front of the queue, she couldn't half move for an 80-year-old. Naturally, the bus appeared, just as she was being served. *Rats,* I thought, *what are the chances?* Now I had another decision. I bounded after her into the shop and snatched the card and stamp from her grasp, then dashed out into the open road as whatever bus it was approached. Unfortunately, he wasn't braking, there'd been no-one at the stop, and since the road was a bit of an ice rink, *THUD!* I hit the driver's side and landed squarely onto my back. The bus just carried on up the road, churning all the snow in its wake. *You rotten, selfish pig,* I thought as I lay there in the slush.

Though slightly dazed I wasn't hurt, I felt a tad more embarrassed than anything. I got up and brushed myself down. My arse and sleeves were soaking wet. None of my people seemed concerned, they all just went about their business. Just some idiot in the road. *Sod 'em,* I thought. *Sod 'em all!*

There had to be another way. First I made it onto the pavement. Then I scanned the row of cars that were loosely parked in front of the shops.

Bingo! I was in luck, it seemed, an old schoolmate was sat in a Peugeot, staring blankly into space with a look of availability.

"JOHN!" I yelled.

He didn't respond. I crossed the road and rapped on his window.

"JOHN!" (He wound the window down). "I'll give you a pound for a lift to the office!"

"Sorry, I can't."

"Aw, come on, that's *twice* the bus fare!"

"Get the bus then!"

"Missed it."

"Really? Whose fault's that?"

"Mine, of course, for being too kind! Come on John, a friend in need. A *mate*. What could be more important?"

"The *wife*. Well, she is right now. She's in the butcher's getting the pies!"

John and Pat were unemployed, they ate quite well and owned a car. I knew a few who lived like that. I often wondered how they did it.

"It'll only take ten minutes!"

"Aye, but she'll be out in five!"

Jeez, I thought, *the henpecked bastard, grow a pair, you useless get!*

"Look," I said, "I've got the mail and frankly it's in a hell of a state, but now it's gonna be late as well if I don't get back to the office, quick. You only live a minute away, it wouldn't kill her to walk home, would it?"

"Well, it might, the paths are slippy. Plus, a fall might squash the pies!"

"Aye, aye, alright," I said, "I'll do the same for you someday."

So much for old mates, I thought. You couldn't rely on anyone.

Of course, the next bus didn't show and I didn't get back to the office till twelve. By then I was an hour late, the outgoing mail had long since gone. So had all the others, but they all had cars to get around in. What the hell, I'd tried my best. Occasionally, it wasn't enough.

I opened up a mail sack and prepared to empty my sodden pouches. I was interrupted by sarcasm.

"Not much point now, is there, Eric?"

It was Ed. Creeping Jesus.

"Come on, what's the story *this* time?"

"*This* time?" I said. "*This* time? *Really?* Well, OK, I'll *tell* ya, shall I?"

I told him about the snow in the box, the kids, the buses, the little old lady, I told him about my ex-friend John, I even mentioned the hot cheese slice.

"Eric," he said, "I don't wanna hear it!" There was genuine anger there. "I don't believe a word you say! What the hell do you take me for?"

"A miserable sod with an axe to grind and not a bloody ounce of compassion!" And since he was stood there, looking stupid, I added, "You wanna know something else? You're a *joke* of a supervisor, you haven't a *clue* about this job, you're just a *king* who's stuck in his castle with *no idea* what it's like out there!"

He gasped and stepped back, eyebrows raised. I must have hurt his pride or something. "RIGHT!" he screamed, "YOU'VE GONE TOO FAR! YOU'LL GET A WRITTEN WARNING FOR THIS!"

And off he stormed, in a fury. *Good fucking riddance,* I thought to myself. The less you saw of a man like Ed, the better you seemed to feel, full stop.

I emptied my pouches into the sack. The mail *poured* in, suspended in water. Tough. I arranged the packets and sorted my second delivery.

I flipped the van keys off the hook and slowly ventured back outside. I glanced around at the state of the roads. They were pretty treacherous. I stopped and took a long, deep breath and made a start with loading the van. I slung the mail on the passenger seat. I was *not* a happy chap. If Ed had shown his face again I'd have jacked the whole thing in on the spot and written out my resignation from the warmth of the nearest pub.

However, the day wasn't over just yet. There was a package for one of the schools. This is going to be fun, I thought, and sure enough, outside the entrance, I was smacked on the side of the head with the hardest snowball ever to hit me. If it wasn't solid ice it must have had a rock inside. Something splattered everywhere. I hoped it wasn't blood . . .

But that was it, I lost the plot, the mist descended instantly, and since I'd caught a glimpse of the culprit, laughing and dashing snow from his hands, I chased him up by the dining hall, with all his little mates looking on, and caught him by the anorak hood as the snow began to take its toll.

I was desperate for revenge, but what was I supposed to do? Slap him? Give him a Chinese burn? Twist his arm behind his back? Lift him off the ground by his ears until he started squealing for mercy? In the end I was lenient and simply filled his hood with snow, then slapped it firmly onto his head before scrubbing a load of it into his scalp and stuffing the rest down the back of his neck.

There, you clever little twat!

The kid looked shocked and burst into tears. I left him there without a word. I didn't give a damn if he squealed.

In the end, it didn't happen. No-one came to take me away. It was just as well, I thought, chances were I'd have lost it again and added to the list of charges.

Later, when I'd settled down, I gave the day's events some thought. I was an adult, he was a child, I should have had more self-control. But hopefully he'd learned his lesson. *I* was learning more by the day. Whether you did right or wrong, trouble often followed.

14

Then came Spring and the new tax year. Changes were about to be made. Changes designed to minimise costs and make Royal Mail a lot more efficient. *My* job, it appeared, was safe as Ed's threats never did materialise, nevertheless, despite huge profits, cutbacks were a constant threat as the government bled us for all they could get. Larger offices suffered the most as larger savings could be made. Smaller establishments, like ours, would most of the time emerge unscathed. This time, however, we were a target. Monkton brought us all our mail, and since they had an impossible budget, deliveries to satellite stations were right at the top of their hit-list.

I hounded Ed for the latest news.

"So, who's gonna bring us the mail?"

"The way it's looking, one of us!"

Us? Well, it wouldn't be *him*.

Of course, it put the wind up Jack, who already did the lion's share, but everybody knew the score, since me and Kenny shared the van, the two of *us* were the likely targets. Naturally I favoured Kenny and accordingly he favoured me, but Ed knew nothing about the job, so Mr Stubbs, another suit, was booked to come and sort it out.

Mr Stubbs was only small but had a massive reputation, Dave the delivery driver told us, he was our link to the outside world. If cuts were needed Stubbs would make them, no matter *how* many people protested, and there he stood by the overtime sheets, gleaning all the 'facts' from Ed.

He stood erect and pigeon-chested, like a mini Sergeant Major, hairy ears and heavy eyelids, lower jaw uncomfortably large. What *was* it with these Royal Mail suits? How come they were so unsightly? Granted, *I* didn't look too good but at least I could manage a smile now and then. Fair enough, their jobs weren't easy, budgets were increasingly tight and they got no change from the Monkton crowd, Mr Stubbs especially. Delivery staff, under managers, *everybody* seemed to hate him, Dave despised him, *more* so now he was planning to scrap his overtime run. We all got payslips through the mail and his would always go astray, turning up a few days late with a date-stamp from the arse-end of nowhere. Poor old Mr Stubbs, I thought, to be the focus of all that hate. But he was known for sorting things out, and now he was here, sorting *us* out.

He opened up his leather briefcase, cleared his throat and began . . .

"Well, you all know why I'm here. Mr Thorntree has kept you informed. Needs being what they are right now we're having to scrap our outward deliveries. No going back, we've got our orders, what it means for *you* is that commencing Monday, April the second, one of *you* will have to come down and collect the mail from Monkton each day. Alright, who's it going to be?"

Jack leapt in: "Well, *I* can't do it! *Eric's* got the lightest walk! *He* should get the bloody job!"

"*What?*" I said, "You cheeky get! How do *you* know mine's the lightest?"

"Cos I've done them all!" he squealed.

"Really? When was that, the *'60s?*"

"Doesn't matter when," he said, "I know the lot of 'em, inside out!"

"Prove it then," I countered swiftly, "send for the Time and Motion team!"

I knew they wouldn't go for that. Time and Motion studies were costly. They were trying to *save* some cash not waste it on the likes of us.

"Anyway," I continued as a hush descended on the room, "even if my walk *is* lightest, what about the packet run? Any advantage *I* might have gets cancelled out in the afternoons, I reckon I do *most* round here and you want me to work an extra hour?"

"*Two* hours," Mr Stubbs suggested, "don't forget the second delivery."

Second delivery? Hmm, yes . . . *everyone* had forgot about that!

Kenny finally broke his silence, until then he'd kept well out of it. "Come on Mr Stubbs," he said, "where can *anyone* find two hours?"

Perhaps if he closed his travelling shop then maybe *he* could find the time. Nevertheless my mouth stayed shut and Mr Stubbs was forced into action.

"Right," he said with complete authority, "*you're* the ones that know the walks, so either volunteer right now or *I'll* decide and that'll be that!"

We had to think of something fast. Kenny leapt in first: "Alright! *I* can do the second run as long as Eric does the first!"

I cottoned on immediately, Kenny was a sly old bastard, he was resigned to getting *something* and thus was snatching the easier run. We both had trouble getting up and the first run meant a five o'clock start. Plus there was only *one* run on Saturdays. Why had *I* not thought of that?

Stubbs looked happy. Jack did too. Ed just looked like a stupefied chimp. Everybody looked at me. They had me in a corner.

I tried to delay the inevitable by pointing out there were more first runs, then Kenny offered to do the Saturdays, knowing I'd find them impossible. With six runs up against my five I suddenly had the easier task. Mr Stubbs's eyes met mine.

"Well, what about it, Eric?"

I tried to glean some compensation.

"Well, it's not as simple as that. Think of what it means on paper: dragging my shift an hour forward leaves me short at the end of the day. I'd only have an hour or so for the second delivery *and* the packets. Obviously, it can't be done. Not within my shift parameters. So, unless you're a bloody *Time Lord* or you can think of anything else, pay me ten minutes overtime, for every packet, and it's a deal."

Six o'clock was an early start but five o'clock was taking the piss. I knew I'd have to buy a car. The overtime was badly needed. Still, ten whole minutes per packet was more than Kenny and I ever got. Mr Stubbs just stared at me. We were supposed to be *saving* money.

Yet, surprisingly, he agreed, he didn't try to haggle or anything. Later on I found out why, our budget had nothing to do with Monkton's. Everything was written up and Mr Stubbs marched off in triumph, sorted out in twenty minutes, another success for the Monkton Machete. Plans were drawn and schedules altered. I was now collecting the mail. Pressure was mounting, the noose was tightening. Things were slowly becoming a grind.

15

It didn't take long to find a car, I even had some ready cash. I'd backed a long shot by mistake and made a killing at the bookies. Though not quite a regular, I did enjoy the occasional flutter, especially when I needed things and since they'd shafted me at work I felt in desperate need of a car. Mickey Pratt had one for sale, £600, initially, but one disastrous respray later and £400 secured the deal. Finally, I had some wheels. I was truly independent, a magnificent Ford Capri with paint runs all along the body.

It was quickly put to use, the first day with the brand new schedule. I was feeling so enthused I even had an early night. I woke on time, the car obliged and I got to the office at five o'clock sharp. A tired-looking Ed was there to greet me. His hours had to complement mine. Unfortunately something was missing. The keys to the van. Kenny still had them. Ed couldn't find a spare set either, no doubt Kenny had bagged those too. He claimed he didn't have a phone. "Just another bill," he'd told me. Ed had his address on file but didn't have a Twinage map.

So, Ed got on the phone but Monkton didn't want to know. Satellite support had ceased. This was *our* problem now.

We needed inspiration, badly. Finally I looked at Ed.

"Well," he said, "I knew this fella . . ."

Shit, I thought, *not now you fool!*

"Anyway," I interjected, "how come Kenny's got the keys?"

He stared at me.

Oh, of course. The teatime pillar box collections.

All that we could do was wait. I sat there on my stool in silence. Ed was having none of it.

"Ever fancied *ice hockey*, Eric?"

That was it, I'd had enough, so then I offered up a suggestion: rather than waiting around for Kenny, what if I just drove to Monkton and crammed the mail in the back of the car?

Ed just looked at me. "That's risky."

"Why?"

"Well, it's against the rules, it's overloading . . ."

"It's a solution! How'd ya like to spend all morning fending off late mail complaints?"

He thought about it for a moment. "Hmm, very well," he said. "But be careful and don't tell a soul!" He even said that for such dedication he'd give me a fiver for petrol money.

So there I was on my way to Monkton, contemplating the situation. Was there really room in the car? Would I get away with it? We'd find out soon enough, I thought, at least for the moment I was at peace. Ed was out of earshot and the early morning roads were clear.

I pulled into the Monkton yard and found myself a parking space. There were mail vans everywhere with staff cars parked up in between. Most of the vans were unattended, one or two were loading up. Nobody was loading cars. I made my way inside.

The sorting room was massive, like a warehouse full of sorting frames, with people dashing back and forth, some with letters, some with clipboards. Someone asked me who I was then led me to a pile of mail. A dozen trays and half a dozen sacks. That would fit in the car, no problem.

Next to it was a pile for Twinage.

"Hold on, who's collecting this?"

"*You* are."

"What?"

"*You* are, aren't you? Dave's old run? That's the rest of it!"

Shit. This was news to me. The Twinage mail was never mentioned. Sure there was a schedule but I hadn't thought of reading it. I didn't mind the journey as their office wasn't all that far. What concerned me was the volume, that was quite a lot of mail. I was in a heap of trouble. *Kenny,* I thought, *you'll suffer for this!* Here I was with mission impossible, no doubt he was still in bed! Still, I was stuck with it so off I went to find a cage. No point feeling victimised, I'd volunteered, after all.

I found a cage then loaded it and dragged the whole thing out to the car. I opened the hatch and flattened the seats. This was never going to work. I stood there looking at it all. What I needed was a trailer. Tough, didn't have one so I soldiered on before somebody saw.

I loaded up the Statton mail, first the trays and then the sacks. Then I tried to close the hatch. It was tight but I succeeded. Great. Now the tricky part. The Twinage mail was sat there waiting. All I had was the passenger seat, so I stuck two trays on the floor and then carefully stacked the rest on top, utilising the whole of the seat, in a criss-cross fashion, to aid stability. Then I got behind the wheel. It didn't look too promising. There were still six sacks remaining, sat there, staring up at me. Finally, I did what I could and crammed in four on top of the trays, then jammed the other two, forcibly, in the tiny gap behind the headrests. There, I thought, a job well done. Precarious, but it was in. I should have worked in a sardine factory. Now I had to seal the tin.

I closed the door with the utmost care. Something wavered, then relented. Sacks were bearing down on me while all those heavy trays of mail were wedged in tight against the gear stick. *This is fucking madness,* I thought, I barely had a windscreen left, but hey, it was too late now so I belted up and started the engine.

I was caught by the union man, a spindly fellow, highly strung. He sprinted over towards me, screaming, "HEY! YOU! WHAT'S ALL THIS?"

So close and yet so far, I thought as I ever-so-gently applied the brakes. I wound the window down a touch and tried my best to explain it all . . .

"*Who* are you claiming sanctioned this?"

"Mr Thorntree, down at Statton."

"*That* old fool? JUST WAIT!" he yelled as he sprinted back inside.

Great, I thought, *I'm stuck here now* . . . then I realised that I wasn't . . . therefore, as he disappeared, I quickly slammed back into first and ever-so-carefully eased the clutch, slowly making my escape with all four wheels against the arches.

That was just the start however. There were junctions up ahead. *You* try making a sharp right turn with zero vision to your left. I thought of watching out for headlights, then I realised it was futile, country lanes were one thing but in town you couldn't see the beams. Then I thought of jumping out and quickly scanning the road to the left. No use, it was on a bend, so by the time I'd jumped back in a wagon could have appeared out of nowhere. Only one thing I could do. *Listen out* for oncoming traffic. Not ideal but what the hell. I slowly wound the window down.

I sat there for a moment, listening, not a sound, the road was clear. I quickly started up, pulled out and narrowly missed a speeding cyclist. He whizzed past with an obvious swerve, a second later and he'd have hit me. Luckily he didn't stop. I took a long, deep breath and continued.

Next turn was a left, thank God, and then it was fairly straight to Twinage. However, as I made the turn, the sacks perched up on top of the trays began to waver in my direction. *Shit,* I thought, *please God, no,* but I'd been pretty far from God and they all came crashing down on me and blocked what little vision I had. I hit the brakes and tried to pull over to what I hoped was the side of the road, then just about managed to scramble out with mail sacks spilling out behind me. Four of them now sat on the tarmac. This was starting to piss me off. I hurriedly tried to jam them back in, before the boys in blue turned up. But now I had another problem, one sack simply wouldn't fit. I'd had two on top of the trays with the other two wedged on top of those. Simple. What was going on? The fourth sack wouldn't stay there now. Sack three had encroached a little and now the fourth had an overhang. Well, I thought, it was basic geometry, dragging them all back onto the road. I needed the largest sacks on the bottom, the smaller ones would sit on top. I stared at them as they lay like corpses. They all looked the same to me. I jammed them all back in. Same thing. I stuck the fourth on my lap and continued.

Finally, I got to Twinage. They were out on the pavement, waiting. "Here's your bloody mail!" I said before tooling it swiftly back to Statton.

On arrival, Ed looked pale.

"So," I asked, "they've been in touch?"

"Yes," he said, "and they're not too pleased, that union man's got quite a mouth!"

"Well," I said, "there's no harm done, if they persist deny the lot. It's only one man's word against yours. Treat me right and I'll back you up."

I winked and gave him a knowing smile. I knew he wouldn't treat me right. Of course, I wouldn't have backed him up. Both of us knew where we stood. Still, we never heard no more, the whole charade was soon forgotten. Like the petrol money he'd promised. That was ammunition for later.

16

Monkton was a breath of fresh air, lively and full of colourful characters. Crowds had always put me on edge, but once I'd made an acquaintance or two I soon got used to the hustle and bustle. Bernard Bradshaw managed the floor, an imposing fellow by any criteria; 'Big Bern' wouldn't allow me to leave unless he was sure I had every last letter. People seldom answered him back and if they did it was only once. You had to do it *his* way or he'd hunt you down and give you a bollocking. That was how it was in Monkton, the workload called for maximum effort; volumes were relentless so they needed a big, firm hand on the wheel. Since they were always under the cosh, occasionally, the pressure would show. One guy trashed the office radio, just for playing that Carpenters song. True, they played it every morning, just as the sorting deadline approached, but smashing their only source of joy was *not* the way to relieve any tension. Meanwhile I was making contacts, not because I was sociable, but if Kenny had any holidays in I'd help him out with his business arrangements. Tony covered Kenny's run but he flatly refused to sell any crap, whereas it was fun to me and gave the job a little flavour. It was tough with all that movement and Big Bern breathing down my neck, but I learned the art of covert meetings and soon I'd located the relevant people and every one had a story to tell. The best tales were of Borrowby Flats, a notorious cluster of ramshackle tenements, there the tenants kept pigeons and poultry while goats were pegged to the grass out front and a fourth floor flat was the home to a horse! I went to check it out one day, and there it was, a real live horse, its huge head peering out from the balcony, longing for the grass below. It was like a vertical farm, the council didn't dare to enter, heaven forbid if their giros were late, they'd let the postie get to the top then unleash their mad dogs into the stairwell. One poor soul (it was always a temp) was trapped up there for hours one day; they had to send a search team out, who had to risk their lives to escape as a barrage of bricks rained down from above.

The drive meanwhile was me against nature. Sadly, nature rarely won. I was fond of birds and mammals but schedules were incredibly tight. I'd leave the office at 5 a.m., mostly it was dark and still, but in summer the roads were teeming with life and since I was forced to drive like a maniac some of it didn't survive the van. The first time caught me by surprise, a female pheasant appeared out of nowhere and, as I was going at breakneck speed, it snapped the number plate clean in two. Next, a herring gull smacked off the windscreen, followed by a pigeon or two, but rabbits were a whole other story, some of them had a suicide complex. They'd be sat at the side of the road, their eyes reflecting the morning sun, but as soon as the van came whizzing past they'd suddenly leap out into my path and end their sorry lives in an instant.

One day, on my journey back, the pale sun gently lighting the sky, I hurtled over a minor hill and came across a family of partridges pecking around on the tarmac ahead. Too late to brake, too fast to swerve, I wished them all the best of luck, but *thud-thud-thud*, it wasn't sufficient and as I glanced in the rear-view mirror I saw a couple of lifeless corpses bouncing along the road behind me. Well, I thought, at least it was quick, perhaps a meal for a fox cub or two, but further down the winding road I began to hear a knocking sound which seemed to be coming from somewhere up front. The collision must have broken something. Not *another* number plate? Well, OK, I hardly cared and motored on regardless.

When I got to Twinage they were all stood on the pavement waiting. Doddy asked, "What's that on the van?" His name was Neil but he looked like Ken Dodd. I went and looked and saw a partridge dangling from the radiator, head stuck fast inside the grille, well and truly dead, it seemed.

"Oh . . . *that?* It's my mascot. D'ya like it?"

"Aye, quite apt!"

"Well, it's a warning, see? DO NOT ATTEMPT TO BLOCK THE MAIL!"

When I made it back to base I made a point of showing Kenny. Quickly he produced a knife and sliced the poor thing off at the neck.

"One for the pot!" he proudly proclaimed. "Baked beans à la partridge tonight!" Later, he retrieved the head and started doing crazy impressions.

"H-h-hey, ma hea-, ah sai-, ma hea-, ah sai-, it h-h-hurts!"

Foghorn Leghorn. Look it up. Jack meanwhile was not impressed.

"Since when was Foghorn Leghorn a partridge?"

"WHAT?" said Kenny, annoyed to the max. "Sorry, Jack, I was IMPROVISING, there wasn't a ROOSTER stuck on the van!"

"Not *this* time!" Tony added.

Tony had a valid point. The way that schedule made me drive perhaps it was only a matter of time?

17

Things ran smoothly for a while, the schedule was tight but not impossible. Getting up at four wasn't bad. Even my body clock had adjusted. I had a job, a flat, a car, enough of a wage to pay for it all. There was little chance of promotion but I was *not* the ambitious type.

Then I had a terrible day.

First of all I overslept and got to work a half-hour late. Next the van refused to start, and as I pumped away at the pedal I finally managed to flood the engine. One by one my colleagues arrived as I was waiting for it to dry. Lots of sighing and tutting later and I was over an hour behind. But that was only the start of it, the whole experience had me flustered, by the end of that fateful morning I'd managed to crash the car *and* the van, and later, as I drowned my sorrows, I managed to break my wrist in a fall.

I'm not sure how I crashed the car but I was hit by a baker's van. I'd finished my walk and got in the car and, somehow, pulled out into his path. Luckily the van was empty, cream cakes made a hell of a mess, but Ford Capris were much more robust and though my front wing crumpled as the baker ploughed right into me, the engine still remained intact and I managed to safely park at the kerb. Not so lucky the baker's van; bits were strewn across the road. The driver wasn't hurt, thank God, but still, he was pretty shaken. Technically I wasn't insured, my policy was for personal use, and Royal Mail couldn't acknowledge the crash as we weren't supposed to use our cars. Therefore, once we'd both calmed down, I tried to explain it all to the baker, who agreed, with some reservation, to say we collided a few hours later. Consequently, out in the van, my nerves were feeling a little raw. I hadn't said a thing to Ed . . . he'd have only made things worse. I crept around the roads with caution, making all the proper signals, only to be hit, this time, by an idiot driving a BMW. *Smack!* He'd overshot a bend, whizzing around it far too fast and he'd smashed against the side of the van, which probably, with a degree of irony, somehow kept him on the road. At least he stopped, for that I was thankful. If he hadn't, I'd have been screwed. Still, I was swapping details for the second time in less than an hour. The van was a mess down the passenger side, a tyre was losing pressure too, but since there were only two packets left I thought I may as well finish the round. I trundled along with the window down, getting a few strange looks from the locals. One of them yelled, "YOUR BACK TYRE'S FLAT!"

"AYE, BUT ONLY AT THE BOTTOM!"

Once I'd made it back to base I dumped the van and reported the crash. Ed was aghast but *I* was too. I made my way to the nearest pub.

I woke up sharply in a sweat. Had I dreamt it all, I wondered? Then I felt the pain from my wrist and everything came flooding back. I'd fallen off a bar stool, drunk. My wrist had crumpled underneath. I phoned in sick, went back to bed and slept well into the afternoon.

When I awoke, the following day, it was clear my wrist was a mess. The doctor packed me off to hospital where, after a three-hour wait, they finally put a pot on my arm. The nurse was lovely, wrapping the plaster while smiling at my tales of woe. She probably didn't believe a word but it was hard to believe myself.

My first car trashed within a month; the damage was worse than it appeared. The axle and the frame were bent so I had to sell it off for scrap. I spent my sick leave down the bookies. There was little else to do. The first car came from a winning bet so why not do it all again? At first it didn't seem too likely, five pound doubles didn't work. Ten pound trebles didn't either. I was getting skint quite fast. My last bet was a ten pound trixie, *shit or bust* as some might say. My luck could not have been much worse but surely it would change *some* time?

First up was a greyhound bitch, she looked a cracking bet to me. All she had to do to win was avoid a serious bump, or crowding, or pulling up lame, or being shot. It could happen, gamblers were crazy, sometimes it was *all* at stake. Still, she led all the way, at two-to-one, a steady start.

Next up was an improving horse, a filly, in a one mile maiden. She'd been running well on the soft and I couldn't see anything else to beat her. Nothing much was certain however and so-called 'rags' could often improve, especially when the going changed or the stable had their money down. And this time one of them did just that, at fifty-to-one, a rank outsider, quickening clear approaching the straight with the rest of the pack caught napping behind. Fortunately, it went too soon and the soft ground finally took its toll, with my horse breezing past at the line, at odds of two-to-one again.

That just left another dog, another favourite in the paper. It was in the very last race so there was a nervous wait ahead. A little brindle bitch, trap Six, I chose her not because of her form but as the only wide-running dog she seemed to have a clear advantage. Should the others make for the rails, chances were they'd crowd at the bend, which meant the Six could scoot around them, all the way to victory. It was very wet that day and wet sand helped the wide dogs too, slowing down the overall pace which stopped them swinging a little *too* wide. I was almost there, I thought. What would I go for *this* time around? Something a little sporty perhaps? I was getting ahead of myself.

After what seemed like forever the betting appeared for the final race. The Six dog showed at seven-to-four. Pretty much the forecast price. However, just before the off, she'd drifted out to three-to-one. What the hell was wrong, I wondered, why wasn't everyone *lumping* on? As they loaded up the traps, I couldn't believe it, nine-to-two. *Shit!* Somebody *knew* something, they were lumping on the Three dog instead! Didn't they realise what was at stake? Everyone around me did, the entire place was glued to the screen, my bet was the highlight of the day.

By the time the hare was in motion I'd resigned myself to defeat, but suddenly, as the traps sprung open, the Six dog, unaware of the betting, blasted out with lightning speed and sprinted into an early lead. "GO ON THE SIX!" I screamed out loud as she swiftly scampered into the bend where, as predicted, the others crowded and halfway down the long back straight she'd bounded over six lengths clear. "GO ON YOU BEAUTY, GET ME THAT CAR!" Surely now she *couldn't* be caught. However, stranger things had happened and, sure enough, at the second-last bend, while having maintained a lengthy lead, she suddenly drifted terribly wide, allowing the pack to close a little. In wet sand too, it shouldn't happen, my heart sank as her lead was halved, and as they rounded the final bend with the Six still running far too wide, the Three and Four dogs sailed on past and suddenly now she was back in third! I'd gone from elation to sheer despair, in five seconds flat, I couldn't believe it! Friends, who'd hoped to share in my fortune, were shuffling off towards the door. "NO!!!!!!!" I screamed in desperation, how could this have happened to me? I'd had the race and car in the bag and suddenly it was all an illusion, but *wait*, the drama wasn't over! Halfway down the final straight, the two dogs now disputing the lead, began to move incredibly close, which made them eyeball one another. Maybe they were kennel mates or they had a festering score to settle? Either way, a skirmish ensued, and as they briefly eased the pace the Six dog managed to close again, and with my emotions completely in tatters they all flew past the line together.

It was a three-way photo finish. "Yes! It's got there!" squealed little Gary.

"Well, it *better* have, Gary," I warned, "or else I'll wring your little neck!"

That was rather harsh, I thought . . . it was only his opinion, but the thought of losing a car had left me feeling rather fractious. I was forced to step outside, I couldn't watch the

81

action replay, dog track cameras weren't aligned, the angles were deceptive.

I stood there propped against the wall, chewing on a plastic pen. Then I paced around a little . . . what the hell was going on? The judge was surely taking bribes, we all knew power bred corruption. I just hoped the dodgy cash was favouring the Six dog.

The waiting just went on and on, I chewed and chewed and chewed and chewed, I gazed up at the afternoon sky, hoping for a sign from above. The clouds were slowly drifting by, one looked like a pot of gold, another like a gleaming sports car, then they suddenly fell apart. *OH, COME ON, COME ON!* I thought, I couldn't stand it any longer, ink was leaching into my mouth but I simply couldn't stop chewing that pen!

Finally, the result came through.

"*First* . . . (unbearable pause) . . . *TRAP SIX!*"

"GET IIIIIIINNNN!!!!!" I yelled, punching the air. Five-to-fucking-one as well!!!

I rushed inside, grabbed a slip and calculated all my winnings. Nine hundred and ninety quid. *Marvellous! Almost a grand!* Anne, the cashier, opened the safe and counted it out in front of me. I gave little Gary a scrub on the head before scooping it up with my one good hand and scurrying out of there, back to the flat.

The following morning passed me by and I woke at noon with a terrible headache. I was slumped against the wardrobe, fully dressed but all alone. The flat was in a hell of a state, empty bottles littered the floor, chip shop paper, dirty plates, an overflowing ashtray. The kitchen sink was full of puke, the bathroom hadn't fared much better. Still, first things first, I thought . . . *water, water, water!!!*

After I'd downed my second pint I sat on the couch with my head in my hands. I couldn't remember a single detail, even the pot on my arm was a puzzle. Finally, I thought of something . . . we were sitting in a pub . . . then we all piled back to the flat . . .

yes, of course, the winning bet! Nine hundred and ninety quid! *Shit!* Where the hell was *that?* Then I saw the pack of cards. *NOOOOOO!!!!!* I thought. *Please God, NO!!!* I leapt to my feet and ransacked the room, in and out of cupboards and drawers, the flat was looking worse by the minute. *Think, man, think,* but I *couldn't* think! Just shy of a grand! I felt quite sick. Then I felt it in my bowels. I rushed to the bathroom, yanked down my jeans and *sploosh!* . . . something hit the water. Where the hell did *that* come from? A wad of notes, wrapped in elastic. Quick as a flash, I scooped it out then slammed down forcefully onto the seat.

When the cash was dry enough I counted it out . . . *more* than a grand. I guessed I must have won at cards but the very fact that I'd even risked it proved I was a certified idiot. No more fucking gambling, I thought, I knew I had to replace that car. I walked around enough as it was and I couldn't stand those buses either.

Finally, the pot came off so I scanned the paper for something appropriate. I was drawn to Ford Capris, familiar *and* affordable. I found a standard 1.6, a 'good little runner' for four-nine-five and a jet-black, mean-looking 2-litre Sport, a year younger, for six-nine-five. I went to see the latter model, a neighbour, Jacko, drove me to see it, a stylish beast with alloy wheels, not a paint-run anywhere. The owner took me on a test-drive, I was quite impressed, at first, but soon the steering wheel felt strange and it seemed to pull a tad to the left, on top of which the clutch felt tight so we went to look at the cheaper model.

After a while we found the place. The car stood proudly on the driveway. It was full of glittering charm, metallic sky-blue, with a spoiler. Though the owner wasn't home, his father was, and he could *talk*; we got a good half-hour of spiel and then, at last, another test-drive. This one felt and sounded fine and looked quite clean beneath the bonnet. Jacko seemed to agree with me, though neither of us were budding mechanics.

Finally the father said: "Now listen lads, about the price. FOUR hundred, take it or leave it."

I quickly unwrapped the elastic.

I drove off into the setting sun, blasting the horn as I sped past Jacko. Nothing can stop me now, I thought. Except the empty fuel tank.

18

Then the doctor signed me off, if I could drive then I could work. Shame, it was a lovely summer. I got straight on the phone to Ed.

"Ed, it's me!"

"Whaddya want?"

"Two weeks leave."

"You're on the sick!"

"Not anymore."

Complete silence.

"Well, OK then."

"*Really?*"

"YES!"

Right, where to? Somewhere lively. Somewhere exotic. Somewhere driveable. It was the music festival season. Reading seemed the obvious choice. Ah, the pomp of the Berkshire set. Tea and scones beside the Thames. Four days on a campsite with a thousand scuzzy drunks more like! Terry said he'd come along too, no-one else was bothered, so we bought our tickets, borrowed some tents, filled the boot of the car with booze, then hit the A1 southbound at the crack of dawn the following Thursday.

It was *not* a pleasant drive, my first time on a motorway. What was up with lorry drivers, hadn't they read the Highway Code? Cutting me off, blocking me in, locked to my bumper in front *or* behind. Yes, I know, I could overtake, but as soon as I hit the indicator the one in front would do the same. Then I tried the middle lane. That was only slightly better. Comfortable for a minute or two, then the same thing, only faster. Terry was a nervous wreck, he couldn't even take a nap. Every time I touched the brakes he'd almost leap from his seat in a panic.

We picked up a couple of girls en route. They were off to the festival too. A pair of students, Cassie and Claire, who'd thumbed it from a service station. I told one or two gambling tales while Terry cracked some filthy jokes. The girls just sat there, silently, we were *all* relieved when we got to Reading.

The campsite was a grassy field, the town on one side, the Thames on the other. Beyond it were luxurious houses, the owners must have been mortified. ̄

The girls ran off as soon as we parked.

"What's the matter with *them?*" I asked.

"Couple of lesbians, obviously."

"You reckon?"

"Aye, of course! What else?"

We dragged the tents from the back of the car and rolled them out on the campsite grass. We stood and stared at them for a while. Finally the show began. Terry's tent was inside out, he took a while to cotton on. Mine, although the right way round, appeared to be one of Rubik's creations. We were quite a few pegs short and how exactly did guy ropes work? We looked at all the other tents and did the best we could.

"That was a struggle," Terry said.

"I bloody hope they're waterproof."

"Inside or out?"

"Either way."

The UK wasn't dry for long.

I grabbed a couple of cans from the boot, cracked one open and tossed one to Terry. They were on the warm side but the first one always hit the spot.

"Here's to a drunk weekend!" I said.

"Why aye, let's drink Reading dry!"

We slung our sleeping bags in the tents and headed off to town.

On our way we saw a sign, crudely sellotaped to a lamp post. "FREE BEER, RIGHT THIS WAY!" it said with an arrow pointing up the street. Naturally, we followed it but didn't see anything *like* free beer. Surely there'd be a crowd or a queue? Nothing. Only festival traffic. We looked in all the nooks and crannies, doubling back occasionally, we even asked in a couple of pubs but all we got was dirty looks. Then, as doubts were creeping in and thirst was overtaking our thrift, at last we found another sign, directing us to a corner shop.

There, in the window, was the answer, scrawled in bright red marker:

BUY 6 CANS OF McEWANS EXPORT AND GET AN EXTRA 2 CANS, FREE!!!

"Fuck." I said.

"Let's brick the windows!"

"Now?"

"No, after a skinful."

Too much time had already been lost. We headed for the nearest pub.

The night flew by, as usual, but we were slaughtered soon enough. I vaguely remember a conversation with what I thought were 'working' girls. I begged them not to ruin their lives, they were all so young and pretty. Terry meanwhile had lost the plot and was mumbling incoherently. Perhaps the girls were *not* on the game, I don't recall them saying so, but they just laughed and didn't care and that was all I remember.

I woke up in a hell of a state; thirsty, sweating, throbbing head. On top of which some dirty bastard appeared to be having a piss on my tent. "YOU FILTHY TWAT!" I screamed at him before scrambling out on my hands and knees. Nobody there, just me and the rain. *Oh, right.* Just as well.

The skies were grey and miserable, fairly typical festival fare, what sunlight did emerge from the clouds just hurt my eyes and made things worse. I crawled back under canvas and began to fish for my little white tub. I found it under my sleeping bag, along with my keys, cash and wet wipes. Terry must have heard the rattle. He would rarely miss a trick. "Can *I* have some?" I heard him moan. I downed a couple and slung him the rest.

The campsite flanked the main arena, this is where the bands would play. A wristband was required for entry, branding you a separate species. They were acquired in a special tent which acted like a cattle mart; they snatched your ticket, grabbed your arm and then clamped you like a criminal. The queue was unbelievable, meandering like a human snake, a damp and miserable one at that, without any obvious way around it.

"Fuck *that* for a lark!" said Terry. "What's the time?"

"Opening time."

We turned around and hit the town. The bands would have to wait.

The streets meanwhile were paved with people, festival-goers in the main, with locals weaving in and out with an air of disapproval. We sauntered along, hungover and wet, blocking access to the shops, the more impatient ones among us spilling onto the busy road. We passed another queue of people, stood outside a chemist's shop. Most were propped against the wall, looking worse for wear.

I gave a tap on Terry's shoulder. "Lucky you're with *me*, my lad! Lack of preparation, see?"

"Whaddya mean?"

"Ah, forget it."

We found a pub and went inside. Every single seat was taken. It was barely 11 a.m. Reading was an action town!

"Right, whose round is it?" asked Terry.

"Yours."

He frowned. Stupid question.

"Didn't I get the last ones in? Tell ya what, we'll toss for it."

"No," I said, "go toss on your own!"

"Already have. Back in the tent."

"Look," I said, "stop pissing about! *I'm* not getting the first ones in!"

I hadn't a clue whose round it was but this was the day's first battle of wits. A moral victory at this stage could have set me up for the day ahead. Terry cracked and got them in. Bottles of course. Best in a crowd. If you knocked one over then at least you didn't lose the lot.

We found a space in a dingy corner, behind a table of biker chicks. Six of them, all hair and leathers, sipping at their pints of stout. I sat on the floor against the wall. "Good ideaaaaahhhhh," Terry yawned. He slid his John Lennon glasses off. "So, what's the plan of attack?"

"Well," I started, taking a slug and feeling all the better for it, "*you're* not bothered about the bands . . . so, I guess it's up to me?"

"Right."

"Well, the bands are good but *I'm* not standing around in the rain."

"Not to mention the wristband queue."

"That's what I was on about!"

"Oh! So we'll sell our tickets and get completely bladdered instead?"

"Let me think it over," I said . . . "aye, that sounds good to me!"

So that was it, the weather had won, we'd have to rely on the juke-box now. That and the beer and the Reading characters. We could still have lots of fun.

We sat there on the floor for a while, taking the occasional swig, quite content to pass the time until we pulled around a bit. From our position on the carpet most of the room was out of sight. All we could see was a mass of legs . . . table legs and female legs. The female legs were very nice, each pair finely clad in stockings, chunky leather boots at one end, skimpy-looking skirts at the other. We sat there soaking up the view. There was nowhere else to look. Finally the girls got up so we quickly scrambled onto their seats.

"This one's nice and warm," I said.

"This one's nice and damp!" said Terry. He got down on his hands and knees. You couldn't take him anywhere.

After a while a tout walked in. They'd been trading on the streets. Tickets were going for ninety quid. Ours had only cost us sixty.

"Any tickets?"

"Aye," I said. "Seventy quid!"

"Sixty-five."

"We've heard them going for *ninety*, mate!"

He smiled and gave me seventy.

"You want another one, pal?" asked Terry.

"Yeah, I'll give you sixty-five."

"What?" he said. "You gave him seventy!"

"OK, seventy."

"Seventy-five!"

"Your mate was happy with seventy, *pal!*"

"Aye, but he's a fuckin' *mug,* you'll still make fifteen quid on the deal."

"So will you."

"So, that's fair!"

Terry had a valid point and yet I prayed he wouldn't win. I was one-nil up thus far, a fiver would have levelled it. The tout tried hard to stand his ground but Terry wasn't budging either and after a bout of verbal tennis the tout began to weaken.

"Look, alright then, seventy-five."

"No!" said Terry.

"What?"

"No way! Seventy-five was fair back then but, sod it, I want eighty now!"

"*What?*"

"Tell ya what, we'll toss, a gentleman's agreement, *right?* If *you* win it's seventy-five, if *I* win it's a nice, round eighty."

Reluctantly, the tout agreed.

"Call," said Terry.

"Heads."

Tails.

The tout coughed up the eighty quid. Damn. I was two-one down!

By one o'clock we'd livened up but everyone else had mellowed out, thus we left for a livelier place and found one in the very next street. I hit the bar and soon found Terry chatting away to an odd-looking couple. Terry was giving it most of the chat while they just sat and soaked it up. The guy was forty-five or so, short and thin with greying dreadlocks, battered leather jacket with a rather sullen-looking face. The girl meanwhile looked half his age, cleaner, smarter, very pretty; jet black hair in a tidy ponytail, bare midriff, pierced navel.

"Crackin' belly-button ring!" said Terry.

"Thanks."

"Look, I got one too!" He yanked his t-shirt out of his jeans, unleashing his rather ample beer gut. "Belly-button rings, ponytails, we could be soulmates, you an' me!" He flung an arm around her waist. She smiled a little nervously.

"You call *that* thing a ponytail, a tiny wisp on a shaven head?"

"Ah," said Terry, "service at last! Thank you kindly, my good man!"

He grabbed the bottle, took a swig and then carried on with his chat-up routine. "Right," he said with eyes of lust. "Let's get down to the nitty-gritty! *You* look like the kinky type! *Bondage!* Whaddya think of that? I can give or take y'knaa, there's *nothin'* like a nice good thrashin'!"

They were gone in less than a minute.

"What were you going for there?" I asked. "The seats, a shag or a punch in the face?"

"The seats'll do, but well, y'knaa?"

Then more pubs and much more beer until the last place kicked us out. I'm not sure it was closing time but they kicked us out regardless.

I gazed along the street in a haze.

"Terry."

"What?"

"Which way's home?"

He squinted his eyes but couldn't see much. Off with his glasses. No improvement.

"Oh, you fuckin' *bat!*" I said.

"Charming. Anyway, bats are cute!"

"Fair enough, you fuckin' *mole!*"

"Moles are . . ."

"Jesus, just forget it!"

"How's about we follow the trend, there must be more of us festival types?"

"Er . . . aye . . . probably . . . aye . . ."

"Right then, it's decided."

We looked for a trend but couldn't see one. People were flowing this way and that. *Everyone* looked like festival types. Oh, well, back to the drawing board.

Then I had a brilliant idea. "We were camped by the river, weren't we?"

"Aye, I guess . . ."

"Well . . . that's it!"

"What?"

"It must be downhill, right?"

"Why?"

"It's the river thing, innit?"

"Whaddya mean?"

"Rivers 'n' valleys! Gravity, Newton, all *that* bollocks!"

"Fuckin' A! Lead the way!"

And off we went, downhill I hoped, with clouded minds and bursting bladders. Terry would drift out into the road but otherwise he behaved himself. We found the campsite easy enough, my reasoning had worked the oracle. Now we just had to find our tents with a thousand or so to choose from.

"How did we manage to find them last night?"

"Can't remember."

"Me neither."

"Split up or stay together?" asked Terry.

Eventually we agreed to split.

I walked around for hours it seemed, tripping over endless guy ropes, getting burned by campfires, having slanging matches with all and sundry. Luckily nobody wanted a fight. I'd have settled for directions. All I found were the portaloos, which helped, but I wasn't home.

Then, at last, I got a break, I recognized my craftsmanship, a sawn-off 2-litre lemonade bottle, perched on top of a sturdy twig. My urinal. Oh, what joy! Somehow Terry had beaten me back. I heard him snoring away in his tent. I crawled into mine and slept . . .

The next day was a Saturday, I woke at noon with a raging thirst. I gazed at the river but that was silly. I made my way to town instead. I sauntered back with a six-pack of coke, a four-pack once I'd reached the tents. I opened yet another can . . .

"Oooh, aye, can *I* have some?"

Terry crawled from his tent on cue. I stuck a can on top of his head.

"Cheers, Big Ears."

"You're welcome, Noddy."

He drained it off in one.

He sat there looking terrible; without his specs he was Kermit the Frog. With them he was more like Scooter. Me? I was Fozzie Bear.

Once we'd braved the portaloos we discussed our options over a burger, finally settling on a day trip, London wasn't all that far. We hopped aboard the first train there and hopped back off in half an hour. Off we went to find refreshment, only to be stopped by a Scotchman.

"Hey, hey, excuse me, boys."

"Why, whatcha done?" I asked.

"Oh, great, an English voice, the first a've heard all afternoon! Listen boys, a'm in a fix, a've gotta get back hame tae Glasgae. It's ma wife, y'see boys, she's been rushed tae hospital, suddenly! The trouble is, a've rushed masell an' cannae seem tae find ma wallet! Anyways, tae get back hame, a need tae raise a bit o' train fare."

"Oh, I see, St. Mark's or St. Luke's?"

"What?"

"Y'know, which hospital?"

"St. Mark's."

"Aha! I made it up!"

"Y'what?"

"I made the fucking thing up! There's no St. Mark's or Luke's in Glasgow, certainly not hospitals, so off you trot or I'll call the polis!"

And off he went, on to the next.

We found a pub, a quiet one. Steady away. No real rush. I made for the bar and ordered the drinks. Soon it was a bit *too* quiet.

"Right," said Terry, "where to next?"

"Howzabout the British Museum?"

"What? No way! Howzabout Brixton?"

"*Brixton?* What do they have in Brixton?"

"Riots!"

"That was *ages* ago!"

"I've always wanted to go to Brixton."

"Fair enough, Brixton it is."

I finished my drink. "You hungry yet?"

"No, but I need the bog, to drop a log, the size of a dog. I may be in there quite a while. Whereabouts ya gonna be?"

"The chip shop at the end of the road."

"Which end's that?"

I pointed it out.

"Save me some."

"Not hungry, eh?"

"I'm just about to make some room."

With that in mind I bought some chips and wolfed them down in the afternoon sun. I licked up all the little scraps. Terry could buy his own bloody meals. I ended up with an empty carton without a single bin in sight. Luckily there was a bookies next door. They had bins on every wall.

I sauntered in and ditched the crap, the place was full with the Saturday crowd. Right, I thought, I'm in here now . . . plenty time to catch a race. I grabbed a pen and scanned the screens, the 3:15 at York was due. I checked the field and got a surprise, there it was, Eric's Dream, my favourite horse at four-to-one! This was no coincidence, the Fates were clearly guiding me. I rushed to the counter and scribbled a bet: *Eric's Dream, £20 win.*

I got it down with time to spare and scanned the paper on the wall . . . *my* horse had the better form as well as having the perfect name. Today's race was an easier grade and the opposition didn't seem much. Billy Carr was booked to ride but even *he* could win on this one. Billy was a senior jockey, known for using the same old tactics, running tight against the rails as logic deemed it the shortest route and stopped the horse from drifting wide. However, this would give him problems, mostly towards the end of the race where, as the overall pace increased with everyone jockeying for position, he'd often find himself hemmed in, unable to make a decisive move. He'd scream at all the other jocks to give him a bit of racing room, but these little men were seasoned pros and also wanted to win, sometimes, and often he'd be stuck on the rails until the race was all but over. Well, it was too late now, I'd made the bet and that was that, so I parked myself in front of the screen as thirteen thoroughbreds raced away in a thunderous pack of heaving muscle.

Billy was wearing bright blue silks, I couldn't see him anywhere, I scanned the pack from front to back . . . nothing . . . not a hint of blue. What had happened? Had he fallen? Had they left him in the stalls? Had they got him *in* the stalls? Did I have the right damn race? The commentary was little help, it never mentioned Eric's Dream, until, at last, as the pace increased and they dashed around the final turn, I caught a sudden flash of blue, right there, behind a wall of horses. *Shit!* That was Billy alright, trapped against the rails again! I must have seen it a thousand times! What the hell was wrong with him?

95

"*And as they head towards the straight it's Summer's Lad by a length and a half . . . Eric's Dream is travelling well but there seems to be no way through at the moment . . .*"

All around me punters were fuming: "*Look, he's facking done it again! Cam on, you little swoine, get aaht! I got a bleedin' maankey on this!*"

It didn't help, it never did, he couldn't hear us screaming, he just sat there waiting for a gap that rarely ever materialised. It wasn't till the final furlong that the bulk of the pack had collapsed, but Billy boy was *still* hemmed in, with one horse blocking his path up front and another upsides him, cutting him off; a clever trick but a legal one, providing the horse ran straight and true, and all these boys knew Billy well and knew *exactly* what to do. With all three horses at full pelt there wasn't time to switch around, and even if there was, so what? Billy would *never* do such things, but *wait*, there seemed to be gap, or was there, it was hard to tell, the only thing for certain was that any move he could possibly make was going to have to be *right this moment*. Billy knew, we all knew, there was no point second guessing, so he gave his mount a crack of the whip, a vicious one for such a small man, and as the place reached fever pitch with everyone yelling at the screen, he drove it through with all his might as they bore down on the winning line.

Yet another three-way photo. *No-one* seemed to know who'd won. It was the 1990s and yet cameras *still* weren't on the line. We would simply have to be patient. *Jesus,* I thought, *why do I bother?* Couldn't I win a fucking thing without being made to sweat for it? The whole place seemed to grind to a halt as the punters stood in a mess of uncertainty, some were lighting cigarettes while others had slumped down onto their seats, unable to *think* of another bet unless they had the winner of this one.

Finally, the result came through: "*First, number 3, Eric's Dream . . .*" A cheer went up from every corner, Billy Carr had redeemed himself!

It was a muted cheer, however, we'd all observed just *how* he'd won, and sure enough, just seconds later, a Stewards Enquiry was announced. A mournful groan went up in response as everybody feared the worst. Gamblers were a hopeful crowd but also experts in defeat. Had there *really* been a gap? *Yes, of course* . . . well . . . perhaps. Again, we just had to wait. Stewards Enquiries took forever.

Quarter-to-four and still no outcome. Suddenly I remembered Terry. *Rats!* What the hell was I doing? I'd been in there half an hour! Where the hell was *he* by now? Should I show my face or not? I thought about it for a moment . . . hmmm, it was quite a quandary . . . if he'd still been on the bog then, great, he'd be none the wiser but if he'd made it to the chippy, surely he'd have checked the bookies? No, I thought, I'll just stay here, that £100 was quite a pull. The chances were I'd lost but as a gambler I was full of hope.

I stood there like an imbecile . . . what a way to spend your time . . . gambling wouldn't make me rich . . . *everybody* lost in the end.

They kept us there till four o'clock and then they finally let us have it:

"*After the Stewards Enquiry, the result of the race has been amended* . . ."

Some of us groaned while others cursed, I tore my betting slip to pieces. *Billy Carr,* I thought to myself, *I really hope we never meet!* I briefly thought of chasing my losses but didn't have that much to spare, and so I legged it back to the pub, just in case I wasn't too late. Of course, Terry had long since gone. *Shit, I thought, what now you fool?* We'd agreed on Brixton but I doubted he'd have gone alone. Then again perhaps he had? Perhaps he thought I cramped his style? Perhaps he was lying dead in the gutter? *Billy Carr, you little twat!*

I made my way to the nearest tube, caught one and got off at Brixton. Once I'd surfaced on the street I found the nearest pub and entered.

There sat Terry, bottle in hand, waving it like an imbecile. I tried my best to look indignant. "Where the hell did *you* get to?"

"Here!" he said with a well-oiled grin.

"What's the idea of that?"

"Well, I sat on the bog for what seemed like an age, then after, when I couldn't find you, I just thought you'd got sick of waiting and made your merry way to Brixton."

"Don't you think I'd have checked the bogs?"

"I suppose, but then you didn't!"

"Yes I did!"

"I didn't hear ya!"

"Well, you must've already gone!"

"But why weren't you outside the chippy?"

"What? Shit, well I dunno, I had a slash around the back. You checked?"

"No, I never thought."

"Right."

"Right, so how did you find me?"

"Psychic powers, my friend." I said.

"Psychic powers my hairy arse!"

"I *knew* that you were gonna say that!"

I bought a pint and a bottle of brown, necked the pint and sat right down. Everything was back to normal. There we were, sat in a pub, slowly but surely getting drunk.

The rest of the night was a bit of a blur. Terry and I lost touch again. I do remember the train ride back but nothing much of the Brixton pubs.

I woke up feeling rather queasy. Thankfully my head was fine. Something didn't smell too good. I decided it was me. Terry meanwhile had made it back, his boots were sticking out from his tent. He refused to wash at festivals, etiquette or something, he said. I thought about the river again but there was an indoor pool in town so I filled a bag with a few essentials and weaved my way off-site.

The queue outside the pool was short, considering there was a festival on. Then I realised it was Sunday, maybe they were all in church? I bought a ticket, found a cubicle and peeled off all my three-day-old clobber. I scrambled into a pair of shorts. My first priority was a shower.

The showers were just outside the pool, as the dressing rooms converged. It was an open-plan affair, I grabbed the only one that was free. It was full of festival-goers, everyone looked a similar age and we all just stood there, washing our parts, as floods of scummage slid down the drains. Mostly it was long-haired women, hands stuffed down inside their costumes, giving their pubes a furious scrub, it felt like a puritan's cleansing parlour! I was spellbound, it was hypnotic, all those furry muffs getting seen to, all that soaping around and around, their nether regions all of a froth with streams of residue flooding their thighs. Inevitably, something stirred. *Shit,* I thought, *please God, no!* I turned around to face the wall and prayed that nobody had noticed. Think of something else, I thought, I tried to think of Terry naked, no use, I was full-on hard and it wasn't relenting any time soon. I dropped the soap and got out of there, pretending to adjust my shorts, then quickly dive-bombed into the pool before they came to take me away.

Eventually, I softened up and finally began to relax. It was very peaceful in there, the showers had been more popular. I found a raft and clambered on and stretched out leisurely onto my back, my arms and legs dangling free, the water warm and comforting. Instinctively I closed my eyes and began to dream of a better life, cast adrift on a tropical ocean, not another soul for miles. Occasionally a friendly fish might come and nibble at my toes but, other than that, it was nirvana . . . I was drifting off to sleep . . . then *BZZZZZZT!!!* What the hell was that? Suddenly my eyes sprang open. They were wanting people out? Surely not, the place was empty! Where were all the coloured lights, the ones that matched your wristband colour? And what about the *festival* wristbands, wouldn't it get a bit confusing? Nothing, I could see no lights, perhaps they wanted *everyone* out, perhaps our collective dirt from the showers had somehow managed to clog the drains?

Next I knew I was underwater, both feet scrambling to find the floor, the shock had made me gasp for breath and my lungs were suddenly full of liquid. I was in a state of panic, flapping about like a gibbering idiot, all I wanted was some peace, yet here I was, Eric Peagerm, drowning in the shallow end!

Thankfully it didn't last and seconds later I found my feet. I made my way to the side of the pool and dragged my carcass onto the ledge. My legs were dangling in the water, which was pulsing up against them. Then it clicked, *a wave machine*, and a *buzzer* was meant to be adequate warning?

Later, back at the campsite, it was raining again, though not very hard. Terry's boots were still sticking out so I gave him a friendly kick on the ankle.

"So, what happened to *you* last night?"

He stirred and groaned, as if he was wounded. "Missed a couple of trains, didn't I? Trying to chat up a Japanese student."

"Any luck?"

"Nah, not likely. Don't think she could understand me. If she did she wasn't impressed. I promised 'the biggest bang since Hiroshima'!"

"Well, I've been up the pool and, on the balance of things, I'm fresh. Come on, get yer arse in gear. The pubs are open in half an hour."

He crawled from his tent like a country wino, strewn with bits of grass and straw.

"I've lost my wallet."

"What? You sure?"

"Aye," he croaked, "I reckon so."

He checked his pockets and searched the tent but couldn't find it anywhere. Drunks were always losing things. I must have lost a dozen wallets.

"What's inside?"

"Just me card, some other junk, a couple of notes. I've got a pocketful of change but it's the card I'm worried about."

"Can't you ring and cancel it?"

"Got the number? No, me neither."

"Try directory enquiries."

"What's the point, I've got no details!"

Tragic but it wasn't the end, "Well," I said, checking my pockets. "I've got twenty left to spare, we won't go hungry. Where'd ya lose it?"

"At a guess, on the train. I kept my ticket in there an' all. I couldn't have boarded the train without it."

"Course you could, but never mind. Let's consider the possibilities: if you lost it on the train, we can try the railway station; if you lost it back in town, we can try the local cop shop; if you lost it here on site, we can try the lost property tent; if you lost it back in London, then we're fucked."

"You mean *I'm* fucked."

So, we checked the lost property tent. Zero wallets. What a surprise. We checked the cop shop, the railway station and anywhere else that was open en route. Same result. Not a thing. Not that we were expecting much. There was nothing else to do but pool our cash and go and get pissed.

We ended up in a crowded bar, full of life, a party atmosphere. I was served by a good-looking woman, around my age, with a North-East accent. Later she was sat alone. On a break, I assumed. I left some unfortunate soul with Terry and joined her at her table.

"Alright? I'm Eric."

"Sharon," she said.

"Howdya end up here then, Sharon?"

"Work." she said.

"Work? Oh really? Couldn't you get a job back home? We're crying out for barmaids, y'know, especially *attractive* ones . . ."

"Aye? Well, I *manage* the place and this is where the brewery sent me."

"Well, you must be good at managing, half the other places are empty."

"Aye, we're doing alright just now, not much time to relax, but still . . ."

"So," I asked, "how *do* you relax?"

She fixed me with those big brown eyes. "The same way as everyone else, I reckon."

I was glad I'd had that shower.

Sadly, it would never happen; though she finished work at midnight, it was barely eight o'clock and we only had a fiver left. Billy Carr was such a twat. Still, there were cans in the car and thus we tramped off back to the campsite, fully determined to polish them off.

We made a fire and cracked two open.

"I propose a toast," said Terry. "To Reading . . ."

"And to missed opportunities."

"Whaddya mean by that?"

"Forget it."

It got dark and the fire was low. I went to scrounge a few dry sticks. I could still hear bands on stage so most of the campfires were deserted. On returning, Terry was done. He was snoring away in his tent. *Wendy fuckin' Lightweight,* I thought. I grabbed a can and stoked the fire.

I was joined by a trio of drifters, young, long-haired and seemingly high. Simon and Suki, they were a couple, and Emma, who was Suki's mate. With four cans left I shared them out and found that they were unemployed. Far too poor for festival tickets but rich enough for a good stash of weed. We talked and drank, they lived in Windsor. Did they know the Queen? I asked. "Nah," said Simon, "posh old bitch, I'll burn that castle down some day!"

I told a couple of tales of Terry who snored away, obliviously, then Simon and Suki started necking . . . I felt old at 27. Then I looked across at Emma, she was staring into the fire, glassy eyes reflecting the flames, a certain sadness in her face. Bleached blonde hair, wild and carefree, pixie nose, dangly earrings; silver studs in both her eyebrows, frumpy grandma dress, but stylish.

"So, Emma," I finally asked. "Here on your own?"

"No," she replied, "my boyfriend's knocking around, I think."

"You *think?*"

"He likes to do his own thing."

She turned around and then I saw it, the bruise, just behind one eye.

"He did *that?*"

"Yes, he did."

"He does it often?"

"Yes, he does."

"Why put up with shit like that?"

"Well, who knows, perhaps I like it?"

"Fancy joining me in the tent? *I* can rough you up if you like?"

She glared at me. I wasn't funny. I'd spent too much time with Terry. Everyone got up and left. The festival was over.

I crawled from the tent the following morning. It was pissing down again. Puddles of water everywhere. Time to go, before it got worse. I leapt to my feet, awakened Terry and quickly we dismantled the tents. We stuffed the whole lot into the boot then slammed it down and got in the front. But there was a problem. Quite a big one. We were stuck in an ocean of tents. I couldn't see a clear way out. It looked like we were going nowhere. All that we could do was wait, until the others began to leave. We glared at them as they packed their stuff, resisting the urge to sound the horn. A car or two were getting stuck, their rear wheels spinning around in the mud. Most were having to get out and push. Not too pleasant in the rain. Terry sat there smiling, unaware it could be *his* turn soon. Finally a path was cleared. Time to make a move.

I started up and moved off slowly, carefully weaving through the debris, aiming for the line of traffic queueing for the exit gate. I tried to keep a steady pace, on muddy ground you need momentum. *Come on fella, keep it up*, I gently pleaded with the car. But then some numbskull thwarted me, stumbling blindly into my path, and I was forced to a grinding halt in the middle of a dodgy patch. I slowly tried to move again but the rear wheels made that whirring sound. I looked at Terry, knowingly. He sighed and clambered out.

"Rock me back and forth, alright, and when I get your rhythm . . ."

"Aye."

So he rocked and then I hit it. Nothing. Didn't move an inch.

I got out and looked at Terry. He was completely covered in mud. He took his glasses off to clean them. It was impossible not to laugh. Quickly I resumed my seat and Terry tried to join me, but I dived across and locked the door. "Don't you *dare* get in like that!"

"He stood up straight and glared at me. "By the way, your spoiler's broken."

"You were pushing on the spoiler?"

"Aye."

"Oh, for heaven's sake!"

I got out to investigate. He was right. Well, almost. Some of the bolts had broken loose so I wrenched them off with all the others and tossed the whole thing into the back. Then I reassessed our predicament. It was dire. Too much mud. We were going to need some help. I looked around for possible assistance.

There was a carful right behind us.

"Any chance of a push here, lads?"

"One condition," one of them said.

"Right," I sighed. "Whaddya want?"

"Nothing, just a simple trade. We help you then you help us."

"Fair enough. It's a deal."

I darted back behind the wheel.

Terry, wiser than he looked, grabbed the frame of the passenger door. The others assembled at the rear, hopefully, to give their all. In second gear I eased the clutch. We wavered but began to roll. The rest of it was a stroll in the park, I nudged into the exit queue which, luckily, was barely moving, stopping and starting to let us in on the firmer ground of the boundary road. Then it was time to return the favour. We got out when the traffic stopped. Our rescue crew were sat in their car. Only two of us pushing this time. They floundered in the very same spot. Too much weight and not enough muscle. I knocked on the window and beckoned them out. To my amazement, they refused. By this time *I* was covered in mud and the exit queue was moving again, so *fuck it* I thought, I gave them the finger and left them there to mull it over.

Off we went, soiled and exhausted, stopping only to change our clothes. Terry found a roadside bin and stuffed his muddy shirt inside. I tried to jam the spoiler in, like everything else, it didn't fit. I tossed it wildly into a field and resumed our journey home.

19

At work, nothing much had changed. Ed had bought a water bed. He raved about it constantly. "It's magic for your sex life, folks!" I watched him shuffle across the floor and found it hard to believe he had one. Still, I was a fit young man and *I* didn't have one either.

I crept in through the door one morning, Ed was stood there ashen-faced. The water bed had sprung a leak and flooded half the bedroom.

"Let me guess . . . stiletto heels?"

"No, Mary doesn't wear them."

"What about you?"

No response. He simply wasn't in the mood.

By this time sorting up was a chore, the mindless repetition bugged me. Volumes were increasing too, the junk mail firms were flourishing. Meanwhile conversation was stale, assuming anyone spoke at all. I wasn't much of a talker myself but the lengthy periods of silence were becoming unbearable, even for me. Kenny tried to lighten things by airing a few embarrassing tales, which helped, until Ed chipped in and suddenly we were back to square one. The same old stories, over and over, the ferreting one, the scrotum incident. They were dull the first time round but by the umpteenth you were climbing the walls. If he'd served in World War Two they could have sent him off to Hitler, he'd have shot himself much sooner, if not he'd have seen to Ed. We had to think of something different, something Ed knew little about. We passed a few ideas around and finally settled on TV trivia. Ed would rarely watch the box as Mary liked to watch the soaps, therefore we assumed his knowledge wasn't quite as deep as ours. And so it proved. During quizzes, should he offer up a question, mostly it was from the '50s, some of us weren't born back then. The '60s were a problem too: "Name the very first Doctor Who," which brought the entire place to a halt as we all just stood there scratching our heads.

"I can see him!"

"White-haired bloke!"

"I know him, I know him!"

No, we didn't.

The mail was rather late that day, God knows how it looked on the overtime sheets.

Then I spent a week on the wagon. I was feeling quite lethargic. There was aching in my kidneys and my guts were playing up. Consequently life was dull, I did have records and the TV, but laid up on the couch at night was hardly what you might call living.

I was sat one Saturday night, watching some old mindless junk, bemoaning the fact I was stuck at home when I should have been out there having fun. I mulled it over for a while and decided that the job was to blame. What I needed was a change. Something more fulfilling.

I was interrupted by the phone.

"Hello?"

"*Is that Trimley Club?*"

"Sorry, no."

"*Are you sure?*"

I looked around me. "Quite sure, madam."

Then a pause.

"*What's your number?*"

"Double-eight one, five double-zero."

"*That's the Cluuub!*"

"No, it isn't! Come on over and see for yourself!"

"*Loook,*" she slurred, "*I was told that the number was eeeasy to remember. All it is, is eight-eight-one and then the number of days in a year.*"

"Yes, it is."

"*So it's the Club?*"

"No, it isn't!"

"*Why the FUCK not?*"

"Probably, my silver-tongued minx, cos there aren't five hundred days in a year!"

And that was that. There I was, making all these glorious plans and a drunken female phones out of nowhere and makes me forget the whole damn thing! It wasn't till the Monday morning that I was able to raise a smile. Ed had just returned from Morocco with badly-swollen testicles. We all just stood there chuckling, he didn't divulge the entire story, but Kenny tracked me down in the street and gladly told me the rest of it.

Apparently, a kid had stopped him and asked him if he knew the time, and when he'd flashed his expensive watch, the kid had kicked him in the nuts, which felled him, as it often did, then dragged it from his bony wrist before legging it down the nearest alley.

He'd also got his Masonic ring.

"What Masonic ring?" I asked.

"The one he got from the Masons, y'know?"

"No, I don't."

"Didn't I tell ya? Well, he had a Masonic ring, and should he ever end up in court, he'd simply have to flash the thing and the judge would let him off, scot-free. Whaddya think?"

"I think it's bollocks."

"I dunno . . ."

"Of course it is! Everything he says is crap! He's living in a fantasy world!"

Still, it was food for thought, so why not wind him up one day? I waited for a quiet spell then tipped the wink and off I went.

"Has anyone seen the paper this morning?"

"No."

"Well, this drunken driver, knocked a pensioner down in the street."

"What did he get?"

"A suspended sentence."

"Probably a Mason, then."

"A Stonemason?"

"A *Free*mason."

"Whaddya mean?"

"Oh, y'know, those Mason types are everywhere! He'll have stood there, up in court, with one of those 'Masonic rings', it's one of their secret signs, y'see?"

"Oh, like those silly handshakes?"

"Aye! He'll have flashed his knuckles, both hands gripping tight to the dock, then once the judge caught sight of his ring, the bastard would have let him off!"

"Oh, I see. *That's* how it works?"

"Aye," I said, "of course it is! They do a lot of charity work but most of that's just subterfuge! When they're not in their pagan robes, sacrificing chickens and goats, they're prancing around in frilly pants while their mates are getting away with murder!"

"That's despicable!"

"Terrible!"

"Shocking!"

"Who the hell do they think they are?"

Ed just stood there, silently.

He rarely spoke to me after that.

20

Our first auxiliary then retired. I had been our only second. He was replaced by Jobe Carter: *"The more pallatic he became, the more he looked like Michael Caine."* Jobe was just what the office needed, the life and soul of *any* party. He was always rolling drunk and thus we had a lot in common. Mad? Often. Loud? Usually. Fun and games? All the time. With Ed or Jack my face would drop but it always lifted when Jobe walked in. He'd worked at a brewery for twenty years and had just received a redundancy package. Not enough to retire on, but a nice amount to have in the bank. He loved to watch old John Wayne movies and if he passed you in the street, he'd yell out: "HEY! YOU! NED PEPPER! FILL YOUR HAND YOU SON-OF-A-BITCH!"

He had the pleasure of meeting Ed on his return from yet another holiday. His bench was adjacent to Ed's. He'd just have to grin and bear it.

"Jobe, guess where *I've* just been."

"The lav?"

"No, the Grand Canyon! It's a stunning place, you know, the scenery, the *size* of it! You'll have to pay a visit some time."

"I'll nip across with my first week's pay."

"You wouldn't believe how deep it is!"

"No? You haven't met my wife!"

"No, but listen, seriously, the scale of it defies description! If you jumped off one of the cliffs you'd die before you hit the bottom!"

"Right. Prove it."

Everyone laughed.

"Really though, the mind boggles! Take a guess how deep it is! Go on, guess! I'll give you a tenner!"

Kenny jumped in: "Can *I* have a go? Obviously I haven't a clue, but if I *do* by eleven o'clock, can *I* have a tenner?"

"Oh, alright."

We all made sure we were back on time to see what Kenny had managed to find. He'd have brought a sackful of mail but no-one gave a damn about that.

Then the phone rang. Ed responded: "Hello . . . no, he's not back yet . . . yes. . . yes . . . OK, I'll tell him."

He put the phone down, gingerly.

"That was a teacher, up at the school. He said he had that figure for Kenny."

Everyone laughed, he'd been on a quest. The farms didn't get much mail that day.

Eventually he sauntered in with a bag of mail and a big wide grin.

"Well then?" asked Ed.

"Well then, what?"

"Just how deep do you reckon it is?"

"Write it down on a piece of paper."

"What? Why? Don't you trust me?"

"No."

"Oh, that's charming, that is!"

"Charming or not, write it down!"

So, he got a post-it note and quickly wrote a figure down. He placed it face down onto the bench. Kenny slid him his own bit of paper. Tentatively, he picked it up. His face collapsed like a makeshift tent. Kenny just stood there, smirking, with his palm held out expectantly.

By that time I was back on the drink, not entirely due to Jobe, but I was feeling so much better, I seemed to have a new lease of life. I'd finish my shift, drive back home and jump in the bath to freshen up, then rustle up a bite to eat before finally trotting off to the pub.

One Friday I was interrupted, just as I was leaving the office. Jobe pulled up in a battered old car. "WANT A RIDE TO THE BREWERY?" he yelled.

"Aye, why not?"

I clambered in.

"Easy shift?"

"Easy enough. How about you, it's been, what, a fortnight?"

"Aye, I'm getting used to it. Getting up's not easy though, and I guess I'm pretty slow, but since I'm on the part-time round I can pretty much potter about as I please."

We drove along at a fair old clip. It seemed his front wheels weren't aligned. The whole car stank of whiskey too and yet I wasn't duly concerned as his driving appeared to be perfectly adequate.

Finally we reached the brewery, a big old building, full of charm. We parked up in the cobbled yard and made our way towards the storeroom. As a previous employee, Jobe could buy his beer at discount. This is pretty handy, I thought, as we walked in through an old stone arch where crates of beer and wine and spirits were neatly stacked in every corner. Jobe knew all the staff, of course, and friendly insults were exchanged, but soon enough the beer was bought and loaded into the boot of his car.

Then we drove around the corner, ending up in the brewery club, where half a dozen men in overalls sat at a table full of drinks.

"Bloody hell, we can't get rid of him!"

"MICK, YOU OWLD BAR STEWARD!" yelled Jobe.

Other such greetings were exchanged while I went off to find some seats. Then followed numerous flagons of ale and dozens of bawdy brewery tales, the fiddles, the hassles, the parties, the women, it sounded like a wonderful place! Their jobs were physical, I assumed, and I guessed they all had livers like coal but you had to pay for life on the edge with scant regard for the state of your health. I wondered about their wives at home, if they had them or even homes, but domestic life was never mentioned, it was all about the brewery.

It was the same the following Friday, Jobe pulled up at the office steps and off we went to buy the beer, except, this time, instead of the club, we did a U-turn in the yard, while everyone kept out of the way, then drove across to the A19 and headed south towards The Smog.

"Where the hell are we going, mate?"

"Clevedale North Industrial Estate."

"Really? What's to see down there?"

"A little club I think you'll like."

Oh aye, I thought, what kind of club? How did *he* know what I liked? Then all of a sudden we screeched to a halt. Thankfully, in an empty lay-by.

Jobe got out and opened the boot then jumped back in with a couple of cans.

"Get a bit o' this down yer neck!"

Well, who was *I* to argue?

We resumed with Jobe at the wheel, laughing and joking all the way, a can of beer in one hand and a slightly bent cigarette in the other.

Then he suddenly let me have it. "Look, these bloody wheels are fucked! They only level out at a ton . . . watch . . ." and he put his foot down. Sure enough, at almost a ton, the wobbling steadily subsided. We were surely going to die but at least the final ride would be smooth.

We pulled up at the Haversham Hill, a run-down pub in the middle of nowhere. Chemical plants on either side and a little junkyard around the back. Shabby was an understatement, it appeared to be falling apart, with wooden windows full of rot and plaster peeling from the walls. A German Shepherd patrolled the roof, a vicious-looking one at that, snarling, pacing back and forth, desperate for a quick way down.

"Bloody hell! Is it safe?"

"Why aye!" said Jobe. "Crackin' place!"

At that point I was *not* convinced. Still, *he* seemed keen enough.

On entry there was no improvement, it was dark and full of smoke, the decor reeked of stale neglect from the filthy blotches on the ceiling all the way down to the canvas floor. Despite all this the place was busy, almost three-deep at the bar, exclusively male, mostly in overalls, some in just their regular clothes but a few in business suits as well.

"WHERE'S ME FUCKIN' GIRO THEN?"

I'd forgot I was still in uniform. Best say nothing, I was a stranger. Jobe hit the bar while I looked for seats.

I found a couple of wrought iron stools which I assumed were not being used, then dragged them off to an empty table, the only one that I could see. I settled down amongst the crowd then looked to see how Jobe was doing. He was stood with two big bruisers, holding our drinks precariously.

"Eric! Over here a second! Come and sort these bastards out!"

Christ. When he did get back I drained mine off and went for a refill.

Then, as I was getting my change, the juke-box suddenly started up, a lively dance track, very loud, and a blonde girl waltzed out onto the floor, shaking her body in time to the beat, clad in cheap black underwear with a can of shaving foam in one hand and a bottle of baby oil in the other. She scanned the crowd as she pranced about, flirting with the guys up front, then another big bruiser produced a chair and she circled around it, waving her arms, displaying her props with a cheeky smile before bending over suggestively and carefully placing them both beneath.

I sat back down.

"This is Rikki!"

Jobe was clearly a regular. Exotic dancers weren't my thing but the beer was cheap and I didn't care.

Rikki rocked away to the rhythm, swinging her hips while miming the words, swirling around the room with abandon, blowing a sweet little kiss now and then. She looked like she was loving it, not so the indifferent crowd, a few would glance up on occasion but most of them paid *no* attention. Rikki shook her stuff regardless, flaunting everything she had, before tearing her bra from her ample chest with the swiftness and skill of a true professional, draping it over the back of the chair so it didn't end up on the dirty floor. Next she reached for the can of foam and squirted a dollop on each of her breasts and continued parading around the room, with a bit more care this time, cupping herself while licking her lips, tempting us all with a sensuous stare. Then she suddenly grabbed some guy, a bald bloke wearing gold-rimmed glasses, and parked on his lap with her chest stuck out, inviting him to perform a massage. What could he do? He was trapped and there was only one way out. He was a man and he had to prove it, especially in a place like this. And so, he adjusted his specs, but just as he was about to reach, our Rikki grabbed the back of his head and, with a nod and smile to the crowd, she yanked it down into all that foam, taking the poor bloke by surprise before working his face around and around as he sat there stupefied and helpless. Then he took his glasses off. The whole crowd suddenly burst into laughter. Wow, *they've* perked up, I thought, as Rikki leapt from his lap in an instant and danced around the room in triumph.

Finally the music stopped, though only for a second or two, and then another track began, this time rather more sedate. Rikki steadily paced the floor, smoothing her breasts with the rest of the foam, gradually turning up the heat as she glided around, surveying the crowd, teasing, playing, carefully choosing. Then she sauntered back to the chair and standing above it arched backwards, spreading her legs and thrusting her hips as she dragged her panties to and fro across her mat of dark brown hair. Everyone was watching now as she slipped a couple of fingers inside, rubbing herself with increasing intensity, pursing her lips, feigning arousal, quivering with eyes shut tight. Then, at last, she ripped them off, leaving her dressed in nothing but heels. She sat on the chair and opened her legs and stroked herself a little more . . .

Then another upbeat track, someone started clapping along, Rikki responded and leapt from the chair and danced around the room again. She grabbed a younger guy this time and dragged him across to the open floor. He smiled but it was a nervous smile. She pointed to the dirty canvas. He obeyed, she straddled him, she squatted down and grabbed his crotch. "THE LITTLE TWAT'S GOT A HARD-ON!" she screamed. Everybody laughed again. Then she repositioned herself and parted her legs suggestively. She ordered him to close his eyes, then open his mouth and stick out his tongue. Foolishly, he obliged as Rikki looked at us, shaking her head, before reaching for the bottle of oil and squirting a huge stream into his throat. A cheer went up from around the room as Rikki threw her arms in the air, then finally she took a bow and quickly disappeared from view.

"Whatcha think of that?" asked Jobe.

"Aye, alright. Pretty funny."

"What about Rikki, isn't she gorgeous?"

"Well . . ."

"Get away! She's *beautiful!*"

Right. Then a thought occurred. "How come all of this is free?"

"Well, it's the location, see? How do you draw the crowds out here? With decent beer and good entertainment. Charging people wouldn't work. Not with another pub down the road."

"What? There's *another* nearby?"

"Aye, the King's Head, not too far. Lots of people work round here. Most of them are process workers, technically they're having lunch."

I drained my glass and waved it at Jobe as Rikki reappeared at the bar. She was back in her bra and panties, the same ones that she'd just performed in.

"Rikki! Over here!" yelled Jobe. "Come and get the drinks in, pet!"

116

He was waving a note in the air. Quick as a flash, she scooted over.

"A couple of pints and whatever *you're* having."

She smiled and snatched the note from his hand.

"Thanks my love, back in a jiff."

And true to her word, there she was.

"Come 'ere darlin'," Jobe insisted, grabbing her tightly around the waist. Then he started pawing her breasts. "What a lovely pair of tits!"

Rikki looked at me and laughed. "He can't be gettin' much at home!"

"Oh, I am, I am," said Jobe, "but a change is as good as a rest, they say!"

Rikki sat between us with what appeared to be a piña colada. Classy girl. Then I asked her, "So, do you *enjoy* all this?"

"Aye, it's a canny laugh!"

"Don't you think it's pretty sad?"

"No, not really. Well, perhaps. It depends on why they come. It's just a lark for most of 'em but sometimes it's a little more. But then it's only *really* sad if this is all the sex they get."

"Don't you feel you're being exploited?"

"I'm the one who's getting paid!"

"*I'm* not paying . . ."

"Whoopideedoo, so *both* of us are happy, right? Look, who the hell are you, a postie or a fuckin' student?"

"Well, I'm a postie but I'd like to think I'm a student of *life.* Don't you think it cheapens sex?"

"Oh, fuck off, it's *cabaret!* Who cares if it cheapens sex? No-one gives a shit in here! No, it's not to *everyone's* taste but no-one's *forced* to come along. It pays the bills and feeds the kids and that's what counts at the end of the day."

She necked the drink and off she went. Then the place began to empty. Soon the Hill had lost its charm. Cheap beer couldn't save it. Since we'd finished ours, Jobe stood up. He tossed the car keys on the table.

"Eric, drive, I'm awa the limit!"

From then on I did *all* the driving.

It became a regular thing, our Friday afternoon sojourn. Jobe would pull up in his car as I was finishing off at work, we'd hit the brewery, load up on beer, then scoot off down the A19 with a couple of cans and me at the wheel.

There were different girls each week, they must have been on a rota of sorts, each one with a style of their own, and we were on first name terms with most. There was Nina, what a woman, big all over but not much fat. She wore a bodysuit, black and sheer, and performed with a range of bondage accessories. She had jet-black curly hair and spoke as if to slash your throat. "Hey! You! Drinks! Now!" She was always in command. We cowered at the crack of her whip but were too transfixed to move away. She always held our attention but we'd have loved her to hold a whole lot more. She did a slow, erotic dance that wasn't really a dance at all, it was more of a masturbation sequence, full of steamy sexual energy, rounded off by mounting a table and smothering her body with oil. She'd be driving us out of our minds, teasing us, fucking us all from a distance. She had everything down to an art, the first at the Hill to induce an erection. Once, having finished her act, they'd had her booked at the King's Head too, and off she went in her stage attire, strolling down the road half-naked, thigh-high boots and a see-through bodysuit, cat-o'-nine-tails slung from her shoulder. Annie was another favourite, slender with a gymnast's physique; her act was fully designed to exploit it, her flesh-coloured leotard hugging her body so tightly there was no need to strip. She would do controlled little cartwheels, handstands up against the bar, she'd do the splits in impossible places and if you ever caught her glance she'd fix you with a smouldering stare. Sometimes she would bend over backwards and walk like a demented crab, her soft little belly thrust in the air, she'd drive us all delirious. Those afternoons with Nina or Annie would lift us for the whole weekend, though some weren't quite as sexy or keen, and one, Christina, hated the job. She probably thought we were all disgusting, not that she ever told us so, she was far too

118

sweet and savvy for that but I sensed she'd rather be scrubbing toilets. Three young kids, an absent partner, endless problems with benefit payments. Yes, of course, she had a choice, but often the options were depressing.

Then, one Friday, afterwards, Jobe took me home to meet his wife. Her name was May, a kindly soul, who looked as though she had her hands full.

"May! You should have seen this stripper!"

"Jobe! I don't wanna know!"

"May though, go on, tell her, Eric!"

"JOBE!!! I DON'T WANT TO KNOW!!!"

She suffered him but it can't have been easy, the drinking, the madness, all it demanded. I could feel her sheer frustration. Poor old thing, she really loved him. I myself had something going, I'd been seeing a local girl, as yet we hadn't slept together, didn't want to scare her off. But then that very Friday night she asked me how I'd spent the day, and being a sucker for honesty, I told her exactly where I'd been.

"*What?* What were you doing down there?"

"Oh, it's just a nice ride out, there's no admission, the beer's cheap and . . ."

"AND?"

"Well, it's a bit of a laugh."

"Oh! Stripping's a bit of a laugh?"

"Sometimes, aye, there's this routine . . ."

"It isn't *sexy* at all then, is it?"

"Sometimes, aye, but hey, so what? It's just a bit of relief, y'know?"

"Aye, I'll bet . . . *hand* relief!"

"It's Jobe's idea, it's his car and everything."

"Does he *force* you to go?"

"Well, no."

"So, am *I* not good enough for ya?"

"Yes! I mean, I don't know yet!"

"But strippers, Eric, bloody *strippers!* Can't you see how it makes me feel?"

119

No, I couldn't, I really couldn't. How could you know how *anyone* felt? Especially the opposite sex. And that, as they say, was that.

Soon we'd seen them all at the Hill, though none could quite match Nina or Annie and even *they* lost some of their majesty once I'd seen their acts a few times. Not that we didn't meet other characters, Mick the Nicker for example, he was a serial shoplifter, the archetypal '50s rocker with greased-back hair and bad tattoos. He fancied himself as a part-time assassin, claiming he'd kill for a hundred quid. We had our doubts about his skills but since he mentioned it every week it was obviously an ambition of his. Sometimes there was a magistrate there, who often gave out legal advice, he came in very handy for some, though Mick would never go near him as he'd sent him down a couple of times. It had always been for theft. Mick was always getting caught. Why he'd never shot him was an all-too-frequent bone of contention. There was also Mental Manny, one of Jobe's more curious pals, a slightly subnormal washing-line thief who seemed to spend a lot of his time in the toilet cubicles having a wank. You'd often see him dashing out, hoping to catch the end of the act, jumping up and down at the back for one last glimpse of naked flesh.

Meanwhile, back at the sorting office, Jobe was making fun of Ed. He would call him 'Mr' Ed, the talking horse from the early '60s. Their end soon became 'the stable' and Jobe would stand there every morning, whinnying and pawing the ground, with what he seemed to regard as his hoof. By this time Harry had retired and Jobe had officially replaced him, most of the year it was just part-time, but he also covered the full-time walks when anyone put any holidays in. So Jobe was now a permanent fixture, much to the annoyance of Ed, except when he caught the equine flu and was ordered to stay in bed by the vet. But if Ed wasn't pleased, Jack would be *livid*. It was me all over again, though I confined myself to beer while Jobe was into the harder stuff. I'd often find him sat on the doorstep, half a bottle of whiskey in hand, attempting to subdue the shakes as I rolled up to the door with the mail. So Jack was bitching and griping again, sullying the atmosphere, and though it felt like déjà vu, except this time with another target, it wasn't just about the drink, he seemed to resent Jobe's sense of fun.

"Come on down the Hill," Jobe said, "we'll buy you drinks and loosen you up! I'll tap you up with the lovely Rikki!"

Jack would always flatly refuse.

The others were invited too, I'm not quite sure how seriously, but Ed didn't trust us, Sheila declined, and I don't know what was the matter with Tony but he'd have always made other plans.

"You can buy *me* drinks," said Kenny.

"You're teetotal!" I suggested.

"Not if all the drinks are free!"

Tight-arsed git, I should have guessed.

But Kenny had his teatime collections and often we would make a detour, Jobe had a brother who lived nearby and now and then we'd pay him a visit.

It was just the two of us, it all boiled down to responsibilities. I had none and Jobe didn't care. We did make quite a formidable team.

21

Then I started having problems. It began with the stupid car. The engine started cutting out and not a soul could tell me why. I'd be happily driving along then suddenly it would grind to a halt. All attempts to restart it would fail and I'd be forced to continue on foot. A duff carburettor was diagnosed but a new one didn't solve a thing. They tried another. Didn't work. Mechanics were a waste of time. They swapped a couple of other parts but all to no avail, it seemed. The stupid car was hexed beyond hope. Ford Capris, I was starting to hate them. Though I did gain quite a physique from pushing that heap of junk off the road, I soon developed a very short temper and I would snap at the slightest thing. It wasn't only Jack or Ed who'd have to watch their step on a morning, random people out on the street would also feel the wrath of my tongue. Then I remembered the kid in the snow. What was I heading for *this* time around? I feared the worst and gave it up. The scrapyard won again.

It was then I was offered a council garage, barely a stone's throw from the flat. Great, I thought. Just what I needed. Offer a blowjob to a eunuch. Still, though the timing was bad I felt as though I couldn't refuse. Garages were pretty scarce and people rarely gave them up. So I went and got the keys and gave the thing a thorough inspection. Yes . . . it's a garage, I thought. What am I going to keep in it? The Royal Mail did have bicycles but only Ben had ever used one and *he'd* received an official warning for butchering it to suit his needs. He'd retained the essential features: wheels, pedals, handlebars, seat; but ripped out all the unnecessary items: mudguards, bell, part of the crossbar, even the front brakes were discarded. I assumed those bikes were weighty, not conducive to all those hills, but buses and lifts were unreliable, maybe it was the safer option?

I discovered three in the storeroom, each felt like they were nailed to the floor. Yes, they were solid alright, they looked like relics from the '40s. Out they came and I gave them a whirl and chose the one with the smoothest ride. I dusted it down and applied some oil. I had transport once again.

There were issues nonetheless, there was a platform stuck up front, but it could only support one pouch and mostly we had two or three. It was best when we had three as two were needed to balance your weight and if there wasn't a third on the bike it made you look incompetent. "Why not use the platform then?" my people would ask on a two-pouch day. I felt as though I couldn't answer, as if my own logic baffled me. Finally, I found a solution, a two pouch day was split into three. Three were much more cumbersome but at least I didn't look foolish. And in winter cycling seemed to help, all that exertion kept me warm; in summer however I found it exhausting, by the time I'd reached my walk already I'd be soaked in sweat and desperate for my morning break. Grinding up those hills was a chore, not that I was too disheartened, there were downhill stretches too and without the expense of running a car I did have more disposable income. Then, one day, while laden with mail and attempting to scale the worst of the hills, who should pass me by in his car? None other than Ben, my predecessor. He was also at odds with the hill, it looked like one of Kenny's creations. Finally we both gave up and stopped at the side of the road for a chat.

"How did you ever make it, Ben? No, don't tell me, get a hacksaw!"

"Yes," he laughed, "it's quite a struggle! Even with a bloody car! How's the old job going then?"

"Oh, y'know . . . still enduring."

"Give it time," he told me, "it took fifteen years to finish me off!"

"So," I asked him, "how about you? Getting much serious teaching done?"

"No, not really," he replied. "Classrooms are like war zones today."

Instinctively I knew what he meant, I'd done a fair few government schemes and one was at a local youth club, down at the Community College. There I'd learned the younger kids had little or no respect for authority. Corporal punishment had been banned. Now they felt beyond reproach.

"Ben mate, if I'd wanted kids then maybe *I'd* have been a teacher."

"I'm a teacher *and* have kids and mostly I've regretted both!"

I didn't have much sympathy, like everyone he'd made his choices. Families were a natural thing but I had one or two reservations. All that heartache and mental anguish, then there was the financial side. I didn't feel it was worth the effort. The single life was fine by me.

But back to the bike, my 'trusty steed'. You can guess who called it that. I preferred my 'weekday friend' as I rarely used it at weekends. Jobe rode in on the 'Six o'clock Stage', reprising Kenny's old role with the van. Saturdays were tough enough, the bike and the hills would have been too much.

One Thursday, as I cycled home, I had a swift one in The Stag. The bike was safe enough outside. Who the hell would want to steal it? Still, the damn thing disappeared and I took the whole thing personally. They *must* have known whose bike it was. No-one else had such a relic. They'd have done me for negligence if it hadn't been found in a ditch nearby, but even though I felt relieved, in general, I was furious. And then I got some information, I was told, in confidence, that the village idiot had been spotted, riding it up and down by the church. Then I came across his giro. Right, I thought, I'll teach the twat, and wrote on it, in marker pen, with big, bold letters:

BIKE THIEVES MUST DIE!

Imagine my horror when later that day my source revealed she'd made a mistake. She'd somehow got her names mixed up and I'd terrorised an innocent person. I felt sick. What was I thinking? Who would do a thing like that? Then his mother came and grabbed me, threatening to have me sacked. She screamed at me, incessantly, I had to try and calm her down. I pleaded with her, "listen," I begged, "it's just a case of mistaken identity!" Finally, she did relent, she must have sensed my deep regret, but afterwards I got the feeling bikes were just as bad as cars.

22

I had some money in the bank. Not enough to buy a car, but with a bit of luck, I thought, the bookies might just help me out. They didn't, I was out of luck and quickly 'some' turned into zero. There was nothing else to do but curb the drink and save.

Halloween had come and gone. Bonfire night was a minor diversion. I was bored. Very bored. Only one thing left to do. Out came the wellies, out came the bike and off I went one Sunday morning, a five mile journey through the fog towards the magic mushroom field. It was dark when I set off but light enough when I arrived. I picked as many as I could then made my way back home.

I spread the mushrooms out on card then placed them on my storage heater, an old thing full of thermal bricks, the only source of heat in the flat. Next, I removed the debris, all the bits of grass and insects, often there'd be a maggot or two, things you wouldn't want to eat. Once sanitised I found a bowl and put a handful in the fridge, then grabbed my bag of football gear and scampered back outside.

After the match and a couple of pints I left the rabble in the pub. The conversation wasn't much, but even if it had been I had more important things to do. I had a bath, towelled off, then slipped into some nice clean clothes. I grabbed the mushrooms from the fridge and settled on the couch.

I tossed a couple into my mouth, trying my utmost not to chew. They didn't have a pleasant taste. I washed them down with bargain booze. My stomach wasn't happy, it was often tricky having fun. I forced them back with lots more beer until the bowl was empty.

Soon enough they took effect, it started with a sense of uneasiness, I could hear peculiar sounds which seemed to be coming from every corner. I got up and went to the bathroom and gazed down at the toilet bowl. The water sparkled up at me. I trashed it with an arc of gold. Back in the living room things were happening, everything was coming to life, the walls had started undulating, the carpet was a riot of colour. I slumped back down in a heap on the couch and was swallowed by an immeasurable softness, I began to tingle all over as objects started gently flickering right at the edge of my visual field. I felt a grin come over my face, the TV made no sense at all, the people were spouting gibberish as the psilocin rifled through my brain. The faces seemed familiar but they were all dressed up in period costume, running around, shouting and screaming as if the world were about to end. Then a face appeared that I recognised, it was that Australian chap, his head suspended in the sky against a most intense blue background. He would often make me laugh, a journalist, a satirist, and there he sat with an enormous smirk which only seemed to encourage my own. Then I suddenly lost the plot. *What's all this, what's happening now?* A sinister-looking woman in black was mooching around in a dreary courtyard, acting all intense and mysterious, like some gothic melodrama. Then a sports car hit the screen and raced towards the edge of a cliff, but it wasn't a cliff, it was more like a rooftop, what was a sports car doing up there? I grabbed the remote to change the channel but all the numbers were upside down. *Oh, to hell with this,* I thought, before dragging a pair of shoes from the cupboard and ending up on the path outside.

Which helped, as it often did, I suddenly had a sense of freedom, the air was cool and all was still and I felt a soothing wave of relief. I took a stroll between the houses, they stood tall like cardboard cutouts, neon lights at every window shimmering in the gentle dark. Street lamps towered up above me, glowing with angelic halos, cars approached me silently then roared past with an explosion of noise. I wandered out of the village, dreamily, gazing at the moon and the stars, the trees seemed fresh and full of detail, all the leaves began to smile. Humanity was full of shit. Nature wasn't, it was marvellous, only taking what it needed, laughing at our pitiful lives. But humans were a part of nature, weren't they, really, maybe not, we *were* comprised of the same basic elements, yet we seemed so out of place. Perhaps we were a cosmic joke, created by some god-like comedian, so that truly intelligent beings could watch us all make fools of ourselves . . .

I was back at home by midnight, brain still buzzing merrily away. I slid from my shoes, leapt on the bed, then lay on my back and closed my eyes. Immediately fractals appeared, flowing from one form into another, colours lurid and fully fluorescent, figures emerging from all that geometry, burning briefly then melting away . . . webs were forming, twisting and turning, I was falling and then being caught, then more bright lights, a fairground perhaps, but no, it was more like Vegas; vibrant casinos with doors swinging open, faces of demons beckoning me . . .

By two I'd lost all hope of sleep. Most days I'd get up at four. If I was still spaced out by then I'd simply have to phone in sick. But slowly I returned to normal, with the help of a coffee or two. I had a wash, got dressed and shaved and made it safely to the office.

I was full of zest that day and had a smile for everyone, but sure enough, it didn't last, and by the time of the packet run the elation seemed to have worn off completely. I was suddenly feeling tired, my concentration was starting to wane. I pulled into a cul-de-sac with a couple of packets for Mrs Hyde. I was forced to slam on the brakes. A little sausage dog blocked my path. It simply stood there, motionless, while staring at me with its huge, dark eyes. I sounded my horn but it wouldn't budge. I sighed and clambered out of the van. It wasn't there, it had disappeared. Where the hell's it gone? I thought. I checked behind me, nothing there; I got on my knees, looked under the van. Nothing. I got back on my feet and walked around it, scratching my head. I scanned the entire cul-de-sac. Every garden gate was closed. All the fences were intact, no holes, no spaces, no escape routes. Daschunds couldn't jump a fence; they could barely jump a kerb, a curtain or two were twitching away but there wasn't *any* sign of a dog. I got in the van and sat for a while. I even checked behind the seats. Surely there was *some* explanation but what it was I hadn't a clue. The world was full of strange anomalies, fish-falls, poltergeists, UFOs, though most phenomena could be explained, some things simply defied all reason. All that mattered was *my* reality, not that *it* made too much sense. And off I went in a bit of a daze, forgetting all about Mrs Hyde.

23

The festive season came and went. January was a non-event. But things improved in February with the Shrove Tuesday Ball Game at Sedgeworth. Hundreds of people, yelling and screaming, running around the village green, kicking what looked like an oversized cricket ball, back and forth, for hours on end. The game had rules and a final objective but mostly it was mob-driven chaos, dating back to Medieval times when things were much more simple and violent. Should you want to win the game, and the ball itself, the only prize, you had to 'alley' it in a stream and then fight your way back up to the green with the rampant masses intent on stopping you. Naturally, you needed mates, and lots of them, to attempt such things, but if you had, and you succeeded, you passed the ball through the bull ring, thrice, then everybody could relax. It was a riot, literally, but quite good-natured on the whole, the entire crowd would respect the traffic and even the cops kept out of the way. You'd see them overlooking the green, monitoring proceedings, with their radios on and their fingers crossed in the hope that nothing serious would happen. Sometimes there'd be a broken window, occasionally a leg or two, but mostly it was all good fun and everybody went home happy.

And, of course, there was lots of drinking, running around was thirsty work. I was no exception since I'd saved up quite a bit of cash and felt the need to have some fun. Quite a lot as things turned out, I don't remember getting home, or getting to work the following day, or the drive to Monkton, or anything much. What I *do* remember is the journey back with all the mail. I was slowly sobering up. I recognised the car in front. It belonged to Mr Fry, the supervisor down at Twinage. Their gaff was a tiny place and didn't have accommodation. He was just as late as me yet driving as if far too early. Didn't he realise going too slow was just as bad as going too fast? The Twinage road had twists and turns, tricky at the best of times. Overtaking wasn't easy, in the dark you risked your life. But I was far too late to amble and far too worse for wear to think, so as we met a decent stretch I moved out for a glimpse beyond him and, as I couldn't see any lights, I hit the gas and went flying past. "SEEYA!" I yelled as I sped away, taking the next bend like a pro, then all of a sudden a cat-like figure flashed out into the road ahead. I yanked at the wheel instinctively and swerved across towards the verge, I managed to miss whatever it was but the front wheel failed to miss the kerb. *Shit,* I thought as time stood still, clipping the kerb at speed was bad, but just as I'd managed to straighten up and believe I'd gotten away with it, the steering wheel spun out of my grasp and the van careered across the road. There was nothing I could do. This was it, my final folly. I was in the hands of God. Time to say goodbye. I could see the fence and the telegraph pole both rushing towards me, ominously, I closed my eyes and clenched my teeth, then . . . CRUNCH! . . . THUD! . . . it felt like flying . . . CRASH! . . . BANG! and a final WALLOP!!! Suddenly everything was silent, everything was completely black . . . I felt numb . . . disembodied . . . So, this is death? I thought. It wasn't bad, I felt at peace, no pain or anything, just a void, until I slowly became aware of the tension that had gripped my face. Sensing it confused me, I was surely dead a moment ago, but now I wasn't quite so sure, the soul should not have *physical* feelings. Maybe I'd survived the crash, no matter how unlikely it seemed? Only one sure way to tell, relax and try to open my eyes . . .

First thing I saw was the roadside verge, slightly raised, a stone's throw away, which had a vaguely familiar look, although I couldn't quite understand why. Next I saw the hole in the fence and the telegraph pole now resting against it, blue sparks dancing into the air where the cables kissed the bare barbed wire. Then I felt a breeze on my face, the van no longer had a windscreen. Judging by the evidence it seemed my time wasn't up just yet. I pondered for a moment on the delicate nature of my existence, this was not the first time I'd escaped what seemed like certain death. Was it just coincidence or did I have a destiny? Who could tell? First things first, I had to extricate myself.

Something pressed against my arm, it seemed to be a wooden fencepost, quite a big one, thick and square, impaled between the seat and the handbrake. I was up to my waist in mail, infused with shards of shattered glass. My seat belt still remained intact. No doubt it had saved my life. I reached down and unhooked it then I tried my best to open the door. Not a chance, it wouldn't budge. I couldn't reach the passenger side. The only thing that I could do was scramble out across the bonnet, not a dignified escape, but I managed it, eventually, and ended up on a bare ploughed field.

I turned around to survey the damage. The van was in a right old state. The only things that hadn't been wrecked were the steering wheel, the dash and the seats. The roof, the bonnet, the doors, the panels, all were trashed beyond repair. I checked my body as best as I could. No pain or blood. It was a miracle.

Though my legs felt pretty weak I made my way towards the road. There I saw a hazy figure, silhouetted against some headlights. It was good old Mr Fry, standing with his hands on his hips. "Tsk, tsk," he muttered out loud. "That's what you get for driving too fast!"

"Just stay there," I told him as I clambered through the gap in the fence. No chance, he was smarter than that and legged it swiftly back to his car. "I'll phone up for a rescue team," he said as he scrambled through the door. He drove off, pretty sharpish for once. All that I could do was wait.

I sat on the verge and stared at the field, gazing at my stricken vehicle. Soon, Doddy pulled up in his van. He stood there with his hands on *his* hips.

"Tsk, tsk . . ."

I glared at him.

"Come on," he said, descending the verge.

"Come on *what?* Leave it, it's fucked!"

"Aye, I know, but we need the mail!"

What? Why? It made no sense. I'd been sitting there in a daze. Then I realised who I was. *Hmm, yes, I suppose we did.*

We managed to get the back doors open and made a start with unloading it all. Some of the trays had broken apart so we stuffed the mail into empty sacks which Doddy had thoughtfully brought along. We slung them into the back of his van, then I went to get in the front.

"Sorry mate," Doddy informed me, "orders are that you wait here."

"Why?"

"*Why?* Why d'ya think? Someone else is coming for *you.*"

"Who?"

"Guess?"

"WHO?"

"Big Bern."

He shook his head and drove away.

Soon enough, Big Bern pulled up. He stood there with his hands on his hips.

What's all this, I thought to myself, *some stupid secret Royal Mail protocol?*

"You alright?" he asked me, curtly.

"Aye," I said, "but look at the van!"

He stood there, rather nonchalant, as he scrawled away with a pen on his clip-board.

"Where *are* we?"

"The side of a road."

"Don't be fuckin' funny, alright? We need a location, an accurate one. The tow truck needs to find the damn thing."

I did my best.

"Right, get in."

He drove me back to Statton in silence. He could surely smell my breath but somehow it was never mentioned.

On arrival Doddy was there, he'd kindly brought us all our mail. They'd separated as much as they could, the rest could follow on second delivery. Bern and Ed then had a chat while I filled out an incident form. Neither of them bothered to read it. Shortly after, Big Bern left. He'd ordered Ed to inform the police but it wasn't *him* who'd trashed the van, so *I* was told to get on the phone and tell them exactly what had happened.

"*Monkton Constabulary, can I help?*"

"Yes, I've been involved in an accident. I was driving a Royal Mail van."

"*Your full name, please?*"

"Eric Peagerm."

"*Are you hurt?*"

"No, not really."

"*Is anyone hurt?*"

"Not a soul."

"*Then why the hell are you calling us?*"

"Because there's a hole in a farmer's fence and a telegraph pole's been smashed in two."

There was a lengthy pause, then a sigh.

"*Very well, we'll send someone out.*"

What a waste of time *that* was. No-one ever did turn up.

Ed just stood there, looking at me.

"Wanna go home?"

"No, not really."

I was shaken up a bit, but running home would have looked quite soft.

The rest of the gang had little to say, they'd save all that for behind my back. Kenny just sat there, rolling a fag. How was he going to get to the farms?

Jobe then grabbed me as we left. "Well done, Eric, well done lad! I was in a state this morning, all that drama bought some time! It meant that I could sit on the steps and have the occasional nip of Scotch!"

I put my hands on my hips. "Tsk, tsk!"

He didn't get it, naturally.

But none of this escaped the public, someone had seen the van in the field. No-one believed I could have been driving, the salvage team were astonished too. Come summer there were scars in the barley, clearly marking the impact zone. "That was down to *me*," I'd say. My life had not amounted to much.

Then the inquest; first the letter; I opened it up:

Dear Mr Peagerm,

With reference to the incident on 24/02/93, it's been concluded, from the report, that you were at fault on this occasion. We consider it careless driving, resulting in the loss of a vehicle, plus some damage to third party property, claims against which are still outstanding. Fortunately, for you and Royal Mail, there are no further charges pending, thus your record has been updated and we consider the whole matter closed. I must take time to inform you, however, that should you incur any other infractions, within twelve calendar months of this date, you could be withdrawn from driving duty.

Yours sincerely,

Chief Traffic Officer.

Well, I thought, it could have been worse. But twelve more months without any incidents? I decided to appeal.

The hearing was downtown in Monkton, a one-on-one with a Royal Mail suit. This one had appeared at Christmas, gifting us with a tin of biscuits.

Off he went: "Right, Mr Peagerm, I have read the entire report, so therefore would you like to explain just *why* you think you weren't to blame?"

Right then, I thought, don't mention the speed or all that overtaking nonsense, focus instead on the cat-like figure that suddenly leapt out into the road.

"I was forced to swerve, y'see, an animal leapt out into the road."

"What kind of animal?"

"Not quite sure, but it was black, a cat, I assume. There's a farm around the corner and they have cats, good mousers y'know, but anyhow, suddenly there it was and instinctively I swerved to avoid it."

"Mr Peagerm, can I assume that you have read the Highway Code?"

"Yes."

"*And* the Road Traffic Act?"

"Which one's that?"

"The current one."

"Erm . . ."

"*Both* explain that swerving shows a lack of control and is dangerous, which means that you should *brake* not swerve. Don't you agree?"

"Yes, in principle. But the whole thing happened so quickly, I had little time to think, it simply leapt out into the road, it's like I said, an instinctive reaction."

"What speed would you say you were doing?"

"I dunno, fifty or so?"

"Fifty or so?"

"I think so, I was focussed on the road, y'see?"

"And, for that particular road, is that a safe and reasonable speed?"

"Yes, I think it is."

"I see . . ."

He paused and gave a little frown.

"Well, at the end of the day, you left the road at considerable speed, contrary to all the guidelines . . ."

"Look," I said, "just tell me this! What would have happened if it was a child? I'd be a *hero* for swerving *then!*"

"It wasn't a child."

"No, but it *could've* been! What are you trying to tell me here? We're not allowed to swerve for *anyone?* Not even *kids?*"

136

"No, it's the law. We all must live and die by the law. Even though it may seem harsh. But you alone were involved that day, so only you can be held to account. It's no big deal, you're not being punished, a mark against your record, that's all. And not for long, so try not to worry. I'm sure that this won't happen again."

"How do *YOU* know?"

"Cause I'm *SURE* you'll take a lot more care in future."

"Will I?"

"Yes."

"Fine then," I said. "Lay the blame on *me* if you want but if *YOUR* kid ever ends up in the road, don't be surprised if I hit him, that's all!"

24

I'd finally saved enough for a car when my kid brother offered to sell me his. A sickly pale-green Vauxhall Nova. Ten years old but a good little runner.

Right away I told him straight: "I only pay £400 for cars."

"*400 quid?*" he squealed with derision.

Big brother won. The car was mine.

Within a week I'd had a bump, I'd nudged it into the back of a van, but it was repaired and it still ran well and I felt a certain sense of relief to have got the first one out of the way.

And that summer was pleasant enough, fairly cool but mostly dry. I wasn't drinking a huge amount and thus I thought I'd venture out and see a bit of the countryside. I caught a couple of music festivals, visited old friends here and there, shuttled back and forth to the beach, without a hint of mechanical trouble. Back at work it was much the same, yet another Christmas passed, followed by my 30th birthday, suddenly I was feeling old. I managed to get a few days off and bravely embarked on a bit of a bender. When I returned, out of the blue, Ed and Mary both retired. I should have been glad, it should have felt good, I should have been dancing in the streets, and yet I didn't feel anything much, I guess, in the end, I'd just got used to them. Ed had been a part of the furniture, stood there in his own little corner, he was like a worn-out couch that you frowned upon but accepted regardless. Now he'd gone it was no big thing, there hadn't been a farewell party, curiously, I shook his hand but I don't remember wishing him well.

He was succeeded by big Dom Smith, a strapping bloke from Tyneside way, and Marjorie, a Yorkshire lass, a much more friendly and amiable pair. They appeared to be more relaxed, despite a bit of caution, initially. No doubt Ed had told some tales but I was sure I'd win them over. Both were in their early forties, they too had just sold a pub. "Too much friction," Dom suggested. "Too many hours!" Marjorie added. Dom was built for running a pub but had a quiet disposition, light brown hair with a thick moustache which spanned the length of his broad upper lip. Marjorie was well-built too with big green eyes and a nice warm smile. Mid-length hair, blonde and wavy, slightly wicked sense of humour. Soon enough they settled in, we told big Dom how *we* did things, and even though a suit showed up to give him a dose of official training, he managed to get to grips with it all while Marjorie took control of the shop. Even Jack seemed more relaxed, we had no need for TV trivia, we could now hold conversations without repeats of insipid old tales which were bad enough the first time round. Better still, Dom was a drinker, no more need to walk on eggshells. Jobe and I were much relieved, the boss was finally on *our* side.

With all this new-found positivity I attended a social event, a Laurel and Hardy 'day of fun', in a town just half an hour away. Stan had lived there as a child, his dad had managed a theatre there and the local branch of the Sons Of The Desert had put together a little tour of all the places that might be of interest. Not that many as things turned out, but there was a film show afterwards, and the group were followed around the town by a pair of Stan and Ollie lookalikes, driving a replica Ford Model-T. I was on the two o'clock tour, it was a Saturday afternoon, there'd been an earlier group in the morning but they'd all skipped the film show and had wandered off on a pub crawl instead. I'd have liked to have joined them as I had the bulk of their films on tape, but then again I had the car, so while there was alcohol on my mind, I tooled it swiftly back to Trimley and made it to The Stag by four. There I spied a crowd of people, gathered in a corner, so I hit the bar and bought a pint and went across to investigate. It was Jenson, an old school mate, originally from Trimley but a family row had forced him to leave and nowadays he lived in Boroughby. He looked wild with all his tattoos, his shaven head and his smashed up teeth; his ears, nose and nipples were pierced, but all that stuff was just for show and I was always pleased to see him. And there he sat with his cock hanging out and half the pub all gathered round, staring at the ampallang, a shiny metal barbell bolt impaled right through the flesh of his helmet. *Ouch!* It was the same all night, in every pub we entered, it was zipper down, out with the junkstick, followed by gasps of shock and horror. It grew tiresome after a while, until he saw me in the bogs, and as he knew I could keep a secret he'd told me how he'd got it done. The piercer had arrived at his house, some biker mates were sat on the couch, and in the most extreme camp voice he'd told him that he needed a hard-on and offered to 'help him out' if needed. He was only joking of course but the bikers must have ripped him to pieces and *that* thought cheered me up no end as his piss sprayed out in a thousand directions.

That night Jenson crashed at mine, his cock had not impressed the girls, then after the footie I drove him home and we parted with an agreement that we'd meet at the Ball Game the following Tuesday. Which we did, another fun day, but Jenson got the last bus home and next I knew I was stood at my door, jabbing at the lock with a key. Eventually I got it in but opened up to a wall of heat. *Whoosh!* I was taken aback, my storage heater was on full power but it had been quite mild that day and in my rush to get to Sedgeworth I hadn't thought to turn it down. Still, first things first, I thought, I needed the toilet, badly, so I emptied my pockets onto the heater, a £10 note and a couple of coins, then opened the bathroom window wide before wrestling with my button-down fly and finally getting some sweet relief. Then I opened the other windows, no point turning the heater down, the thing was full of thermal bricks and the cooling process took forever. And that's when something unfortunate happened. As the heat began to escape and cooler air came rushing in, a strong draught whisked across the room and the £10 note, as if suicidal, suddenly leapt up into the air and plummeted down *behind* the heater. *Rats!* I thought. What were the chances? There was barely a half-inch gap, yet somehow it had managed to swallow what might have bought me a gallon of beer. Immediately I thought of rescue, that old heater was terribly hot, the tenner would never have lasted the night, it might have even started a fire. What I needed was a tool. Something long and fairly thin. A snooker cue! Didn't have one, all I could find was a big wooden spoon, which wasn't nearly long enough, appropriate, but much too short, I really needed more of a gap so that I could get my arm down there. The heater wasn't screwed to the wall, the damn thing didn't need to be, those thermal bricks were really heavy and there were dozens of them inside. So, I spread my legs apart and gripped the heater with intent. Big mistake. As I did, immediately it burned my fingers. *Ouch!* Time for gloves, I thought, I dug some out and slipped them on, then carefully resumed my stance before taking a grip on the heater again. I took a long, deep breath and heaved. It was heavier than I'd thought. The heater moved an inch or two but as soon as I started to reach for the spoon it snapped back onto the wall with a bang. The whole room juddered with the force. It was clearly a bad idea, but I was drunk and beyond any reasoning, therefore I retook my position and braced myself for another attempt. This time I was more successful and almost got the heater balanced, my thighs were taking a lot of the weight but it seemed like *some* sort of equilibrium. Then I reached for the spoon again, which sat on the floor, a little behind me. Equilibrium? Not any more, my thighs detected movement and before there was time to change my mind the whole thing suddenly crashed down upon me. I was pinned to the floor in an instant, heat scorching into my jeans, the weight of the thing was preposterous, my legs were both completely flat and yet somehow twisted around to the left. I had to get it off me, fast, the searing heat was pretty intense, but with the help of a surge of adrenaline, and a subtle twist of the hips, I managed to drag my left leg free, boot and all, from underneath. Now for the right. Almost there, just one last manoeuvre, I thought, and with one boot against the heater, using it for leverage, I began to drag my right leg out and, for a second, I thought I'd succeeded. Not so, I was trapped by the calf. Almost there but not completely. As I'd dragged my left leg free the pressure had doubled up on the right, and since my boots were slip-on affairs, my foot had slithered out this time. Probably a good thing, right? Wrong. Ask a physicist. Once my thigh was in the clear the weight then suddenly shifted again, my boot was wider than my calf and the heater crushed it into the floor. I heaved and heaved but the leg wouldn't move, the adrenaline had dissipated, I felt desperate but weak, the pain was becoming intolerable. The heat, the weight, I began to panic and pounded on the floor with my fist. "HELP!" I screamed. "HELP ME! PLEEEEEASE!!!" Surely *somebody* could hear? Benny lived in the flat below, I'd seen him in the pub that night, but he'd came home a while before me and I'd heard him crashing about down there. Alas, Benny never came and the blistering heat intensified, it felt as though my flesh was *frying*, then there was a blinding light . . .

I awoke in a bit of a daze. The whole room seemed to be full of mist. Not quite smoke but uniform, suspended in the atmosphere. My calf was still beneath the heater. Shit, I thought, I hadn't dreamt it. Curiously I felt no pain, my leg was numb below the knee. Still, no point lying there, time to try again old boy, the chances were I'd starve to death before anyone came to rescue me. I braced myself and started heaving, left boot pushing, right leg pulling, seconds later I was free as the heater slammed against the carpet. *Jesus,* I thought, *that* was easy. Obviously I'd sobered up. I dragged my carcass onto my feet and then looked down at the leg of my jeans. It was blackened, burned to a crisp, which might have explained the misty haze. Then I spied the £10 note that had been the cause of all this palaver. I reached down and picked it up then flopped down wearily onto the couch. Next I knew the buzzer went off. It was Dom, strangely enough. By this time it was 7 a.m., he'd rang a couple of hours ago, but since I hadn't answered the phone he'd drove the van to Monkton himself and picked up all the morning mail. "Give me a couple of minutes," I said as I slowly removed my ball game clothes. My leg felt strange, cold and numb. I stood there staring down at it. Just above my ankle there was a six-inch square of golden crust, slightly weeping at the edges, like a slice of buttered toast. At least it didn't hurt, I thought, nothing I could do for now and soon enough I was sat in the car and on my merry way to work.

Only Jobe was left in there. "I did your mail as best I could."

"Cheers Jobe, I'm sure it's fine."

Well, it would have to do.

Later that morning, after my walk, I popped back into the flat for a drink. All that haze was thickening up. Time to turn the heater off. I collared Jobe that afternoon and we managed to haul it up off the floor. A charred boot lay underneath.

"Well," said Jobe, "it *is* Ash Wednesday!"

Then, at last, I phoned the doctor's but as expected they were busy.

"Is it urgent?"

"I dunno."

"Right then. Friday, five o'clock."

But Thursday came and things had changed, I couldn't put any weight on the leg. It was swollen and very red so I phoned in sick and went back to bed. When I awoke it seemed much worse, my calf was slowly turning purple. I was back on the phone again. "I think I need the doctor, NOW!"

Finally, he did turn up, but wasn't very pleased at all. "This leg is badly infected!" he said. "How long has it been like this?"

"A day or two."

"A *day* or two? Good heavens! This is serious!"

He pumped me full antibiotics then got on the phone for an ambulance.

Next I knew I was sat in a room with Mr Shah at Boroughby General. *Mister* Shah for heaven's sake. Couldn't I have a doctor, at least?

A pin came out and in it went.

"Feel that?"

"No."

"That?"

"Er, no."

"Well, it seems to be burned to the bone. You're going to need a graft, young man."

"Great."

"You'll be assigned a nurse. She'll look after all your needs."

"*All* my needs? Seriously?"

"Within the scope of medical care."

At least I got a room of my own, burns were susceptible to infection. June, my nurse, was excellent and soon she had me settled in.

Mr Shah explained the procedure. Right thigh was the donor site. Strips of skin would be excised and stitched in place to form the graft. Everything would meld and heal to form a brand new layer of skin. Not at all what I'd expected. Interesting nonetheless.

I met the anaesthetist next morning. What a questionnaire he had.

"Why do you need to know all this?"

"To ensure the anaesthetic won't kill you."

NIL BY MOUTH hung over the bed. I hobbled back and forth to the bathroom. Subsequently I missed my pre-med, I was told they couldn't find me. When they did it was time for the theatre. Off I went without delay. They hooked me up to the sleepy stuff, then as they steadily wheeled me in I saw a strange metallic thing that reminded me of a bacon slicer.

Then I was out.

Next I knew I was lying on my back in bed. Nurse June's face was taking form, smiling down on me like an angel.

"Eric? Eric? Are you in pain? Can I get you something, sweetheart?"

"No, not yet, I just woke up. A glass of water for later perhaps?"

144

She brought me a jug and an empty glass and propped me up against a pillow. "Try to be still and stay on your back. That'll help your leg to heal."

Eventually I looked at it. My calf was wrapped in cotton wool. My thigh was wrapped in something too, but it was thoroughly soaked in blood. Completely normal, I was assured. Thankfully I felt no pain. Nothing much of note that is, but one thing that I learned that day was never, *ever*, miss your pre-med. Afterwards was torturous, at first I only felt on edge, but then it just got worse and worse and pretty soon I was all in a panic.

I was desperate to get out. "LET ME RUN!!!" I screamed at June.

"Try to ride it out," she told me.

"How long for?"

"As long as it takes."

Anaesthetic withdrawal, you see. Worse than any operation. All that I could do to curb it was reach across for a set of headphones and sit, for what seemed like forever, shaking my good leg to hospital radio.

Finally I got some sleep and woke up feeling much, much better. After that I was terribly bored. Stupidly, I asked for a bed bath. I was wheeled away to the bathroom and dumped there with a scraggy flannel. Not what I was hoping for, but hospitals weren't there for *that*. The food was pretty good though, I was always last call on the ward and mostly I could have what I wanted, lots of it, and all for free. Then suddenly I was back at home, the graft had 'taken', apparently, I still had quite a way to go, but all I needed was some rest and a change of dressings every day. For this I had a Community Nurse, she introduced herself as Shirley, very friendly, sexy too and she zapped my buzzer every morning. On went the gloves and off came the dressings, the graft was doing pretty well, the donor site however, not so . . . what with the dressing being soaked in blood, hardened blood by the time she arrived, when it finally did come off, enormous chunks of scab and pus would be torn right off along with the bandages. Thus it took a while to heal. I did grow very fond of Shirley, she would bring me medication but also, when I needed it, a little bit of shopping too. Of course, she was happily married and almost a decade older than me, but it was hell, I tell you, when she was messing around with my thigh like that.

25

Two months later I was healed. The doctor signed me off the sick. I did need aftercare however as skin grafts lacked a number of things. No.1: Sebaceous glands, I had to apply a moisturiser; No.2: Pigment cells, I had to cover it up in sunlight; No.3: Hair follicles, that didn't seem to matter much; but what *did* matter, sadly, was that grafts were relatively fragile and wouldn't stand up to Sunday League. My glorious football career was over. Still, it was a talking point, and now I could compete with Jenson, especially when out on the town. Out would come the lotion and I'd dream up some miraculous story, savaged by animals, burned in the war, it helped to add a bit of glamour. Then one day I collared Benny, as he left the flat below. I told him all about the leg. "Jeez," he said, "I bet *that* hurt."

"Well, y'know, it stung a little. Didn't you hear me banging and shouting?"

"Aye," he said, "but I just ignored it; I assumed it was you and Jenson, jamming needles through yer cocks!"

I did see Jenson that weekend and told him all about my ordeal. The scars came out but he wasn't impressed. He had a new tattoo on his back. Then, when I arrived back home, a fridge was standing out on the pavement. All my windows were open wide. Suddenly I felt quite sick. I ran upstairs to check it out and found my door had been kicked in. I quickly scanned the living room but nothing else seemed out of place.

Baffled, I went back outside as Benny came around the corner.

"What the hell's gone on here, Benny?"

"Chip pan fire. That's *my* fridge. The entire block was filled with smoke and no-one knew if you were in. The firemen had to smash yer door, in case you were asleep in there."

Ah, yes, there *was* a smell but why the hell was the fridge outside?

"To dry it out. Water damage. Thought I might be able to save it. Someone's coming out tomorrow to fix yer door and a few other things."

"Right then, cheers."

And off he went.

Karma, I thought, that's Karma that is.

Back at work there'd been a development, Dom had got some canine protection, a lovely German Shepherd named Sam, a cuddly type, just eight months old. He'd failed in his police dog exams and thus he'd been put up for adoption, ending up with a menial job on the fringes of the public sector. Though he did seem bright enough I guessed he'd just been far too friendly, even Jack could pat his head, so clearly there was *something* wrong. He'd watch me as I stood there sorting, waiting for attention, and if I should start a conversation or take part in an existing one, he'd sit there with his ears pricked up, hanging on my every word. Then, once I'd finished talking and carried on sorting up the mail, I'd hear him give a little whine as he shuffled about, impatiently, before standing up with his paws on the bench and nudging me with his big wet nose. I seemed to have a friend in Sam though often he would turn to Kenny, he had female dogs at home and sometimes Sam would catch their scent. Once he tried to mount him and just stood there drooling down his back. "He doesn't know what to do," said Dom, "his instincts haven't kicked in yet!"

"Really? Whose?"

"Either one."

"I think he needs a bit of practice."

"Well," said Kenny, "*I'd* suggest you get him something else for that!"

And he did. Enter: Ella, yet another failed police dog. Not the cuddly type this time but more of a psychotic nightmare. Everyone was scared of her, she didn't seem to like us at all, she wouldn't accept a pat on the head and growled if anyone moved too close. She'd lie there, watching, waiting, as you tried your best to forget she was there, then suddenly she'd sneak behind you and give you a nip on the back of the leg.

"Oy! Dom!"

"Stop it, Ella!"

Sam at least had something to mount. And soon enough we got the news. Ella was expecting pups.

Meanwhile Jobe was entertaining, telling us all of his boozy nights, his place was always pretty well-stocked and Kenny had been paying him visits. Some teetotaller *he* turned out. I myself was rarely involved as six long mornings and one afternoon was quite enough of Jobe for me. Reports then started to filter through about Jobe's performance on the streets. Some had claimed they weren't getting mail till five o'clock in the afternoon. Though he covered the full-time walks, for holidays and the occasional sickness, where the hell he'd been till then was anybody's guess. In the meantime we had a new auxiliary, Bobby Short, a decent chap, who'd married Kenny's younger sister, which didn't seem to matter, at first, but suddenly Kenny's attitude changed and he started telling tales of Jobe, he said he'd seen him dropping letters and stumbling over gates and walls. He also said that he'd been told that lots of mail had been wrongly delivered, and that just put the wind up Jack, who claimed that after a fortnight off there were whiskey bottles all over his walk. Probably an exaggeration but sure enough the word soon spread and shortly after a suit arrived and Jobe was confined to the part-time walk.

I got a call from him one night: "Eric, someone's grassed me up!"

I told him it was one of two. Possibly both. He agreed.

"I don't think I can stomach this."

"Right then, how's your health these days?"

149

"Not too good, dodgy back."

"Well then fella . . ."

"Aye, I know."

But Jobe persisted for a while, till Bobby got a job elsewhere. *Then* he put a sick note in. Little victories were needed. Ronnie Marr was then appointed, quite an inoffensive type, and when it seemed that Jobe was done the part-time walk belonged to him. Which meant we needed a new auxiliary, enter Mrs Pamela Proud, like Ronnie she was fifty or so, but whereas he was quietly spoken Pam was a more of a mouthy old bat. She rattled on about god knows what, ten times worse than old Ed Thorntree, she was just as bad on the streets, she gleaned the gossip and spread it around, whether you wanted to hear it or not, the village grapevine was one thing but she made it sound like sordid central. So, with her instead of Jobe, things were looking bleak again. The trust had gone, along with the laughter, even Sam had lost his appeal. Since his association with Ella he'd slowly developed an angry streak, and though Dom loved having two stroppy dogs, the rest of us just didn't feel safe. We had to stand with our legs shut tight as they wandered around the room, crotch height, and I was nursing a skin graft so it really *was* an uncomfortable time. The atmosphere felt pretty grim, we hardly ever spoke at all, we sorted up in record time in a rush to make it out the door. And then, just as Ella's pups had given us *all* a bit of relief, she'd somehow *devoured* them all one evening. Everything was turning ugly.

26

Down at Monkton the pressure was on. New procedures slowed things down. Every morning I'd have to wait as they struggled through a mountain of mail. I took my time when driving in, I took my time when driving out. Why should nature have to suffer? Let the managers sort it out. Then they had me *weighing* the mail. No-one could explain *that* one. Whatever the weight I shipped it out, a little late, but what the hell. And then they dropped another bombshell, this time it would hit us hard. An overtime ban as Christmas approached. Everyone was up in arms. Christmas *ran* on overtime, the volume of mail was ridiculous. How were we going to clear the decks? Easy, scrap the second deliveries. Back at the office, Jack was incensed. "Twice the work for no more pay!" I felt him but the game was up, we'd had it far too good in the past. I managed a little compensation, telling my people all about it. Tales of moral injustice *did* result in better tips that year.

But after Christmas things got worse, Dom would give us weekly briefings, one week it was the need for economy, next it would be customer service. One thing contradicted the other, there was nothing *we* could do, we did our jobs the same as always, Dom would have to fudge his reports. The economy thing was easy enough, the overtime had gone, job done. Customer service was more of a challenge and customers were little help. One day it was just sheer pettiness, all the lawns were soaking wet, but I was good and wellied-up so naturally I cut across them.

"Oy!" said an angry voice behind me. "Can't you use the bloody footpaths?"

"Aye, I could, but I'd be late."

"So? You only bring me bills!"

I turned around and looked him over, fat, unshaven, middle-aged. He stood there in his tartan slippers.

"Right then, tell me, what's the problem?"

"Look at the state of my lawn!" he whined.

"What about it?"

"Well, just LOOK! Your footprints, all across the front!"

"That's the cost of prompt deliveries."

"*Really?*"

"Aye, it's only footprints."

He was getting pretty worked up.

"I've a mind to report you, son!"

"Do it then!"

And then he did.

Unfortunately, he rang Head Office and I was slated over the phone. I tried explaining the need for economy, but it was customer service week.

So, I started using the paths. Well, one of the paths, at least. Not that it made the slightest difference. After it snowed I heard that voice:

"OY!"

"Jesus, what is it *now?*"

"You've walked across the lawn again!"

"Bollocks!"

"Look, there's your footprints!"

I went back and had a look.

"Right! Look again my friend!" I placed my welly next to a footprint. They were barely half my size. "So, do those belong to ME?"

"Er . . . well . . . I dunno."

"SO, DO THOSE BELONG TO *ME?*"

"Well, they could be the paper boy's . . ."

"Aye, they *could* be, COULDN'T they!"

And then I got another complaint. This time it was Daley Road. Statements from the bank were missing.

What's that got to do with me?

I asked for further clarification. Dom said it was No.12. Ah, yes. No.12. The one who stood and blocked the doorway.

"I assume a *man* complained?"

"Yes, that's right."

"Leave it with me."

"Take it easy, Eric, please!"

"You know me . . . tact and diplomacy!"

I was there in double time. I was looking forward to this. There was a packet for No.6 but I jammed it through her box regardless.

There she stood. No.12. Snow on the ground but the door wide open.

"Nothing today," I told her, "but I've been informed there's been a complaint?"

"Yes, we're missing mail from the bank."

"Is your husband there?"

"What for?"

"*He's* the one who made the complaint, so *he's* the one I need to talk to."

"Oh, I see, well he's in bed, he's been on nights, I can't disturb him."

"Can you go and get him, *please?*"

"NO, you'll have to talk to ME!"

I didn't have to, down he came. "Alright, what the hell's going on?"

"Statements from the bank going missing?"

"Aye, that's right."

"Let me explain: your good wife stands at the door each morning, all the mail goes directly to HER; the bills, the junk, the stuff from the bank . . . EVERYTHING, she gets it ALL. So I'd suggest you go to the bank and get a statement over the counter. Read the whole thing through, with care, then let us know if you want to proceed."

And off I stormed, indignantly, without a word from either of them. We heard no more from No.12 and the door stayed shut, whatever the weather.

27

By now I was completely miserable, everything was such a chore. The work was boring, the managers mad and the customers were *not* my people.

Then we all received a letter:

"Do you have untapped potential? Are you feeling unfulfilled? If your answer is yes, to both, then let us help with our brand new initiative! Come and see us down at Head Office and take part in a relaxed group session. See for yourself the exciting roles available NOW within Royal Mail!"

Most of my colleagues ripped it up, declaring it a waste of time. I however was ready for this, and ended up in a Head Office classroom alongside a legion of other young hopefuls. There we sat with a sheet of paper, describing ourselves, our greatest achievements. What were our future needs and priorities? What did we crave from our careers? I began to express myself, a single sheet was hardly enough, it felt like this was a new beginning, the world was finally opening up. Of course, it was all a ruse, they only wanted a few more managers; sure, there were roles alright, it's just that they weren't that exciting. I had learned the management game while waiting for the mail at Monkton, one or two had opened up as they stood there staring at their clipboards. Managing time and dwindling resources, always striving for more with less; it didn't make much sense to me but fail and you were quickly out. The pressure was relentless, they were always dashing back and forth, making impossible demands in exchange for a torrent of abuse. Who would want a job like that, despised by almost everyone? I knew I wasn't popular, but a Royal Mail manager? Nah, forget it. So, those who felt the same were siphoned off to a smaller room where we were told that, in due course, a specialist from Royal Mail Careers would be in touch to discuss our options.

Nothing happened, naturally. I couldn't be arsed to chase it up. Then I tried the Jobcentre. Surely there was something else? To my surprise, most damn jobs paid even less than Royal Mail did and many paid a whole lot less, there wasn't minimum wage back then. Soon enough I was back in the bookies, ever the dreamer, ever the fool, hoping that I might get lucky and win enough to start a business. God knows what but I had experience, once I'd ran a record label, one of Thatcher's clever schemes which meant, for a tenner on top of your giro, you could start your own little empire and help make Britain great again. Or slash the unemployment figures, depending on how cynical you were. I'd failed of course, but it was fun, I'd managed to put out five E.P.s before falling foul of the stupid tax laws. Still, it was a glorious lifestyle, as the boss you had your freedom, all I needed was an idea, something that could earn me a living. As far as finance goes however my plans were just a little simplistic, gamblers were the same all over, hooked on the theory that if it *could* happen, perhaps, eventually, it might. It rarely did, for any of us, I'd won enough for a cheap car, twice, but a steady business needed more, a whole lot more than fanciful dreams.

Despite all this I ploughed ahead, I only needed a decent strategy, random wagers wouldn't cut it, multiple bets were the only way. I tried round robins, yankees and trixies but any winnings I had were paltry. I would have to up the ante, risky, but what else could I do? I made some careful calculations, yes, it was risky alright, a single bet with four selections would cost the better part of my wage. Nevertheless I soldiered on, I did come close on a few occasions, the difference between success and failure was often just the tip of a snout. Once, I'd have been quite rich if my horse hadn't managed to fall at the last. That sort of thing could turn you to drink but I hardly had the funds for that. Everything was on the line and I quickly fell behind with the rent. Then I fell behind with the rest and soon I was scared to open the mail. Eventually, when I plucked up the courage and worked out just how much I owed, it looked like it was a toss up for whether they simply kicked me out of the flat or cut the electric off beforehand. Then I opened one from the bank. My eyes lit up . . . it was a godsend. How would I like a credit card? *Me? Really?* Sure, why not? No-one had offered me one in the past, or if they had I'd tossed it away. Debt had always been for mugs, but now that I was up to my neck in it, in for a penny, in for a pound. At once, I completed the form. Perhaps they wouldn't bother with checks? Perhaps they would but didn't care? Only time would tell.

28

The card came through and I paid off the rent. Then I paid off everything else. I still had half the balance left and thus my quest could now continue.

Things had not improved at work, the atmosphere was getting worse. Kenny was the main cause as he seemed to be getting later and later when trailing back with the second delivery. He was always full of excuses, none of which were believable, we asked big Dom to make some checks but the only thing that Monkton said was mostly he was late arriving. I was fuming, more than most as I often missed the first dog race, and that was the easiest race on the card, guaranteed, at every track. They'd always give us an early winner, whoever it was that planned these things, safe in the knowledge that sooner or later we'd end up paying it back, and more. For me, it was deadly serious, my frustration was increasing, dogs were giving me grief in the bookies and dogs were giving me grief on the streets. One hound had my knuckles skinned, I'd never actually seen it but it always sat behind the door and snatched the mail before I'd released it, dragging my hand against the letterbox, cleanly carved from cold, sharp steel. Most of them had draught excluders, those damn things were quite resistant, thus you had to use some force which left you vulnerable to dogs. There were rarely people about and you couldn't leave the mail sticking out, so all that you could finally do was have a vicious tug of war and perhaps when the occupants saw the results it would force them into *some* kind of action. Then it was a Rottweiler, the beast was chained to a garden wall, until said chain was ripped from its housing and I was forced behind the shed in a gap too small for the scurrilous brute. When the owner *did* appear it was, "Oh, he's just a softie, really." Yes, of course, I was overreacting, that's why he was chained to a wall.

But the gambling just got worse, I felt as though I couldn't stop; I couldn't think of anything else and barely had a fortnight passed when I'd blown my wages and maxed out the credit card. I would never blame myself . . . it was Kenny's fault, or the job. One day I was so deluded I even blamed the lollipop lady! It was August and very warm, I'd left my jacket in the office, meanwhile I was out in the van, and my last call was to old Mrs Jones who patrolled the busy road near the school. A sweet old girl but boy could she talk, and sure enough, she did just that, I listened but gave her no encouragement, there was a race in less than an hour, a race I felt I just couldn't miss. I'd lost all faith in multiple bets, now it was find one and *lump* it on, the rewards were nowhere near as good but somehow that no longer mattered. I'd been following one such dog, I'd seen it have a string of bad luck, but this time it was dropped in grade and running in the 2:08. But Mrs Jones just prattled on, it felt like there was no escape, and when I did there was no time left so I leapt in the van and buckled up and tooled it back at breakneck speed.

When I got there the office was locked, the door key was inside my jacket. I knocked and knocked but nobody answered. Not a sound from Sam or Ella. Then I realised it was Wednesday, half-day closing, they'd gone out! *Jesus Christ,* I thought. *What now?* Wait it out? It could be hours! I thought of driving the van to the bookies but all my cash was back in the flat. And you *know* where my flat keys were. *Fuck it,* I thought, *I won't be defeated!* So, I jumped back into the van and tore off up the road to Trimley, screeched to a halt, leapt up the stairs and then took a deep breath and booted the door in. It was easier than I'd thought, the fire brigade had done me a favour. Quick as a flash, I grabbed my cash and got to the bookies just in time.

I scribbled the bet as they loaded the traps. The counter clerk just stared at me.

"Come on, COME ON!"

"Too late," he said.

"Whaddya mean?"

"The HARE'S running!"

I glared at him and his smug little face. Where was Anne, the usual girl? Needless to say, my dog won, at four-to-one, I was furious.

And yet such things did not deter me, winners were few and far between, but the dream persisted, I was insane, as long as I was getting paid, at least there was hope, there was always hope. I'd finish work, hit the bookies and stay there till the damn thing closed. Day after day, it was unrelenting, stuck in an endless, pointless routine. Credit card after credit card, once they had you, you were sunk; they'd offer me more and I'd max them out having been accepted without any fuss. Until, one day, they cut me off. Seemingly, I'd reached my limit. There was nothing else to do but get behind with the rent again and anything else I could get behind with.

I was sat at home one Saturday, having blown the last of my pay. My only winner had been a dog, in a six-bend stayers handicap race. And even *that* had been declared void as *my* dog's trap had opened too slowly. Imagine that, too bloody slowly! Because of some electronic mishap *your* dog gets even more of a handicap, yet despite overcoming and winning, some braindead official has made the decision that such occurrences aren't allowed. *All the traps should open at once . . .* Yes, of course they should! So what? The damn dog didn't receive an advantage! *Rules are rules . . .* well SCREW the rules! There were six more days till pay day, I had food but not in abundance. It would be a tough old week, I sat there in a state of defeat. Then I got a call from my father, he was working overseas. My mother was out there too on a visit. He asked how I was getting on.

"Oh, y'know, just plodding along."

That was our average conversation. He was the strong but silent type. Lovely bloke but fairly distant.

"You've remembered the football pools?"

Shit. No. Not *that* week. The collector came at three on Thursday. I'd been otherwise engaged.

Why had I agreed to do it? I was family, I suppose, but why the hell had he trusted me when I couldn't even trust myself? If he'd won he'd surely know, he always used the same ten numbers, family birthdates, mainly, and he always got the English papers.

"Yes," I told him, fingers crossed. The hour that followed was terribly tense. When at last the results came in I checked them off with a sense of dread. He seemed to have a lot of score draws, absolutely the worst case scenario, he was on for a massive win, except that he wasn't, not in reality. One by one the scores came through . . . 1-1 . . . 2-2 . . . it was sickening. He would never, ever, forgive me and I would never forgive myself.

Seven score draws was the final tally. Twenty-two points, three third dividends. Well, I thought, it could have been worse, but what were the dividends going to pay? Thankfully there were lots of draws and the pools were not as they once had been. The National Lottery had begun and the nation were switching to that in droves.

The dividends were announced on the Monday . . . Third dividend: £7.04. I owed my father twenty-one quid. I gave an enormous sigh of relief. Of course, when he phoned that day, I gave him the news with immense disappointment.

"One more draw!" he moaned down the line.

We were not a lucky family.

But the gambling had to stop, I realised it was escalating, should I manage to pay the bills I was left with less than a tenner a week. And then I had arrears to pay. The festive season was almost upon us. I was depressed and full of self-loathing. I had made a mess of things. Still, it was an incredible strain to stop myself from hitting the bookies, especially when payday arrived, the urge was almost overwhelming. Finally, I couldn't resist. Just the one last go, I decided. By the end of that miserable day, I'd blown the lot, my entire pay, with almost nothing left in the bank. The food I had wouldn't last a week, the petrol in the car wouldn't either. And, of course, forget the bills, so when I missed my payment day the council insisted on knowing the reason. What could I possibly say, the truth? It all went on the 4:10 at Fontwell? They were threatening me with eviction. What the hell was I going to do?

Then, at work, word came through that old Ed Thorntree had passed away. He'd suffered a fatal heart attack and never got to enjoy his retirement. I felt nothing, I was numb. I was completely devoid of emotion. Ed had been annoying, true, but no doubt I'd been twice as bad. The following day I felt the same, I drove to Monkton in a daze. There was little food in the flat and the car was sat there, in the garage, the petrol gauge refusing to move. Well, I thought, it's what I deserve as I loaded up the bulk of the mail. The sorters still had a way to go so I stood there with a vacant stare as I watched them work the last few sacks. Then I remembered the football pools. I had the coupon in my pocket. Starving wasn't quite enough, I'd have to be tortured once again when Saturday afternoon came round. Well, the odds did favour me and I'd have had a meal by then, but I'd made many bad decisions, what if it was time to pay? Suddenly I felt the fear, my luck was bad . . . *really* bad . . . all I needed was a fiver, surely I could raise *that* much? And yet where from? A loan was impossible. Everybody knew I gambled. Maybe I could sell some records? No, the record shops were in town and how the hell was I going to get there without any petrol money or bus fare? This was preying on my mind as I circled the frames in a state of bewilderment, shovelling up the last of the mail, Trimley from pigeonhole E-14 and Twinage from next to it, E-15. And then I had a terrible thought. *There may be cash in some of these envelopes.* Well, so what, I wasn't a thief, I may have nicked some stuff as a kid, but now I was, in theory, a grown-up and working in a position of trust! *Borrow it then.* That's no different! Either way, I'd end up in jail! *Only if they catch you, you can always put it back on pay day, letters are always getting delayed.* No! No! I *know* these people! How could I look them in the eye? Then I saw the missort box. J-16. Not *my* people. *Those are not supposed to be*

162

here! And look! There's a birthday card! Someone's sealed it up with tape, there MUST be something hidden in there! I was feeling sick to my stomach. How could I ever think such things? What the hell was I turning into? Yes, I was a no-good gambler but this seemed *way* beyond all that. I wandered round and round the frames, trying my best to talk myself out of it, but that card, that bloody card, that big, fat, juicy, bright pink envelope, sat there, staring up at me!

Finally, I picked it up. It almost seemed inevitable. I slid it under the handful of mail that I'd gathered up legitimately. Then I headed off to the exit. Big Bern stopped me in my tracks. "Follow me, Eric," he told me, before marching me off to the back of the room and showing me into an empty office.

"Put the mail on the table please . . . then, sit down."

I complied.

He took his own seat facing me. I had to hang my head in shame. Then he grabbed the bulk of the letters and shuffled them off to the side of the table. One remained, the bright pink envelope. "Can you explain what you're doing with this?"

"No, I can't."

"I think you *can.*"

Big Bern had a serious face. Then again he always had one. Still, what the hell could I say? Make up some incredible tale and claim it was just a slip of the hand? Lie through my teeth? Plead insanity? No, the bullshit had to stop. I told him the truth and it all came out, I had a serious gambling problem, I blurted out the whole damn story and finished it off with the football pools.

I found the coupon and slammed it down.

"There, *that's* what broke me!" I said.

Big Bern simply looked at me. There wasn't much that he could say.

He made me write the whole thing down. I had to ask for extra paper. Needless to say, I was suspended and left there in the room to stew.

The union man then made an appearance. "Anything I can do to help?"

"Don't be silly," I told him as I waved him off with resignation.

I'd got everything off my chest. I'd come clean and that was the end of it. I had made a stupid mistake. They'd either forgive me or they wouldn't.

Two investigators arrived. Both were dressed in sombre suits. One was tall, dark and depressing. The other was short, fair but friendly.

"Smoke, Eric?" the shorter one asked.

"No, but I could murder a drink!"

"Well . . . tough!" the tall one snapped.

I sensed there was a long day ahead.

Then they drove me off somewhere, attempting a bit of light conversation. I just sat and stared out the window, feeling worse with each passing second.

Finally, the car pulled up. I didn't have a clue which town. We entered a building, climbed some stairs and ended up in an interview room.

Recording began, they read my statement.

"Yes," I said, "that's pretty much it."

Neither of them seemed convinced.

"Come on, Eric," insisted the short one. "*Someone* would've loaned you the money?"

"Maybe, but it's hard to ask. I'm a hopeless gambler, see? Asking *anyone* for help is like showing them *just how* hopeless I am."

"Better than this though," said the tall one.

"I suppose, but I couldn't think."

"Well, you'd better start thinking now!"

And then they both laid into me.

Apparently, other things had been happening, mail going missing, all over Trimley. Statton, Grangeworth and Twinage too. Really? It was news to me.

"Yes, it's an ongoing issue and now we catch you in the act. And you're expecting us to believe . . ."

"Believe what you want! *That's* not me!"

But they persisted, on and on, chipping away until I cracked. What they didn't seem to realise was that I'd *already* cracked.

"So, you think that your arrest will *not* stop any mail going missing?"

"Well, it might, but *that's* not why. Either way, I guess I'm screwed!"

Then I was searched from head to foot. Shameful, but at least I was clean. I asked them if I needed to strip, and though they declined that generous offer, they did say, when they got me back, they'd need to search the flat and the car. They talked about obtaining a warrant. Sod it, I thought, I've nothing to hide and they drove me back with a stop at Statton, to update Dom with the morning's events.

Then they searched my car and garage. Both were clean. Now for the flat. They marched me up with a look of authority, twitching curtains everywhere.

"Lots of posters," said the tall one.

"Yes, but at least it's tidy."

"Like the pelmets . . ."

Jesus, I thought, are they searching the place or buying the place?

Finally, they made a start and pretty much tore the place apart. Drawers were emptied, cupboards examined, they checked beneath the bed and the couch.

Then the tall one emerged from the kitchen, clutching a bag of elastic bands.

"So, would these be *Royal Mail* elastics?"

"Erm, well . . . *some* perhaps."

"Come on, Tom. *That* doesn't count!"

Tom, deflated, returned to the kitchen. Back he came with a different bag. "What's all *this?* Cannabis maybe?"

"No. That's just magic mushrooms."

"*Mushrooms?*"

"Aye, dried for storage."

Both of them just scowled at me. I scowled right back, indignantly.

"Look," I said, "they're not illegal! Well, the drug inside might be, but mushrooms are above the law! Honest! You can check it out!"

They looked at one another, then me. Then at one another again.

"It's up to you," suggested Tom.

"No, it's irrelevant. Let's not bother."

And that was that, some forms were signed to say their efforts had been in vain, and then they finally left me alone with a bit of good, if belated, advice:

"Get some help with the gambling, Eric!"

Then it was just a waiting game, to hear about the repercussions. I was suspended, on full pay, but that was never going to last. I didn't need much help with the gambling, this had stopped me in my tracks. Soon I would be sacked, or worse, and who'd employ me after that? Then there was the word on the street. All the gossips were sure to hear. There was Pam, at work, for a start, and there were dozens of others like her. How would I ever be trusted again? What would friends and family think? And then there was Jack, that bloody Jack, you could just imagine the look on his face!

29

As expected the rumours started and as expected Pam was the source. What I didn't expect however was just how quickly the facts were distorted. That weekend I heard that I'd been the mastermind of a grand conspiracy, I was facing serious charges as, after a raid by a whole gang of officers, *sackfuls* of mail had been found in the flat. A joke, perhaps, but no-one was laughing, save for a few of my so-called friends. I tried my best to put them all straight, but they preferred the sensational version.

Yet my family hadn't heard, no-one had the guts to tell them, least of all me, but what could I say, that I was a fool? They knew *that* much. I kept up with the bills and repayments, easy enough without the gambling, not much spare at the end of the week but the lads had booked a seasonal break and I hoped I might have been able to join them.

Then they sacked me just before Christmas. Lovely timing. Oooh, what's next? A court appearance on my birthday? Well, I hardly deserved any favours.

Big Bern summoned me to Monkton, I retained the right to appeal, but plead for mercy, no, not me, and besides, nobody won such things.

He stood there with a Senior Manager, cold, dark eyes, immaculate suit.

"So, any final confessions?"

"Yes, I quite like Boney M."

And off I went for one last time, pausing as I left the room.

"Any prosecution pending?"

"Not as yet, we'll keep you informed."

Back at home, I had a surprise. A letter from Royal Mail sat on the doormat. P45? That was quick. My sacking must have improved the service.

I was wrong:

Dear Mr Peagerm,

I am very happy to tell you that we've arranged an initial appointment with one of our special Careers Consultants. Please attend at 2 p.m. at Boroughby House on the 18th of January. Please bring proof of your current status and anything else you feel might be relevant.

Yours Sincerely,

Brenda Smith

Head of Royal Mail Human Resources

I was too depressed to be mad. I called her up and politely declined.

So, it was back to the dole, but worse than unemployed, it seemed. Dismissal meant I had to be sanctioned. I'd get £20 a week.
"How the hell can I live on *that?*"
The dole office staff were unimpressed.
"That, Mr Peagerm, is up to you. You might try not to get sacked in future."
All I could do was get on the phone and try to explain my situation; the council, the creditors, all the utilities, somehow, they were understanding. They consumed my final pay but most of my debts were put on hold. But what about the seasonal break? I really needed a pick-me-up.

Off I went to the D.S.S. for a crisis loan on Christmas Eve. The place was heaving, naturally. I took a ticket and sat on the floor. The conversations were revealing, none appeared to involve a crisis. Any guilt was washed away. All I needed was an excuse.

I sat there for a couple of hours until at last they called my number. I was led away to a booth. A stern-looking woman was there to greet me. She could barely look at me. The form was like an exercise book. Only one of the questions mattered:

Why do you need a crisis loan?

I was sanctioned, I was skint, the cupboards were empty, I was starving! Well, that was almost true but *not* the reason I was there. Then I had to wait again. Still no seats. People were desperate. One or two had a screaming fit but they were quickly led outside.

One by one the claims were settled. Some in favour, some against. Mostly it was obvious. Some of the language was insane! They gave me forty quid in the end. Not a lot but the trip was paid for. That would be my spending money. That would simply have to do.

30

Amsterdam, I'd never been. *Cosmopolitan* said the ads. *A city of many different facets*. Most of us had other ideas. Despite the gloom, Christmas passed and I packed a bag on Boxing Day and we drove to Hull in the driving rain: myself, Terry, Hawkeye and Ted.

We bought our guilders at the port and boarded the boat like a bunch of schoolkids. There was a buffet at 7 p.m. so we borrowed a set of plastic chairs and parked ourselves outside the restaurant. Afterwards we made for the bar. A leaflet showed us all the amenities. There was a small casino on board. Good job I was no longer a gambler. Naturally, we all got drunk as everything swayed from side to side. Not enough to make us sick but a toilet trip was quite an experience. Having paid the cheapest fare we didn't actually have any cabins. All we had were communal seats, which weren't exactly designed for comfort. What with the waves and the roar of the engines there was little chance of sleep, there *was* however a breakfast buffet and thus we stuffed ourselves once more before waddling onto mainland Europe.

Customs didn't bother us and we boarded a bus for Amsterdam. The countryside was pretty flat but the fabled windmills were nowhere in sight. Once in town we bought a map and tried our best to locate the hotel which, after a lot of childish squabbling, we somehow stumbled upon by chance. I was sharing a room with Hawkeye, he was tall with short blonde hair, cropped to hide the fact it was thinning, no good for us dark-haired types. We hadn't called him Hawkeye for long, he'd recently had laser surgery, which meant he could lose his specs and zoom in on things from miles away. Terry meanwhile was doubled with Ted, they seemed to be getting along quite well, but didn't want to get *too* close as the first thing they did in their hotel room was to grab a hold of a twin bed each and drag them to opposite sides of the room. Ted was a stubborn, chunky type with a big, round face and a tennis ball haircut; he was always out in the countryside, shooting, ferreting, general slaughter. Once he'd shared a house with Jenson, right in the centre of Boroughby, but eventually he'd moved back home where open fields were plentiful.

And so began a day of sightseeing, mostly inside various bars, but there was a boat trip included, free, which ended with a Diamond House tour. Our hostess was polite and friendly and told us all we needed to know, then once we'd been around the place she led us to a well-lit room where she tried her best to sell us the goods. "Presents for your girlfriends, *right?*" We looked at one another and laughed. We were all too smart for that, or not quite smart enough, *you* choose. More likely we would rob the place, the thought indeed had crossed our minds. Ted had whispered in my ear: *"I've got the door, you grab the stones!"*

"Why should *I* take all the risk?"

"You're the fuckin' thief, my friend! If they're gonna send you down then why not add a bit of glamour?"

That one stopped me in my tracks. It was harsh but it was true. I had a reputation now, my actions just might haunt me forever.

When we emerged, without any diamonds, it was late in the afternoon.

"Well then, what we gonna do next?"

"How about the Torture Museum?"

You can guess who thought of that but lacking options out came the map. When we found it, it was closed. All that we could do was drink.

The bars were on the empty side but still we had a lot of fun; the Dutch were great, they all seemed friendly and spoke much better English than us. The streets were pretty chilled out too, except for all the trams and bikes, and Damstraat was a little edgy, all the dealers badgered Terry who must have looked the druggy type. Of course, no-one had insurance, I could not afford such things but, should we need any hospital treatment, we'd agreed to ride it out and be *carried* back onto the boat, if needed.

We were out well into the night. Terry was the first to crack. "That's enough for me," he slurred and staggered off to find the hotel. The rest of us weren't far behind. We were all a tad unsteady. Hawkeye gazed along the street. I decided it was London.

Ted piped up. "Silly twat! We're in *Amsterdam*, remember?"

Well, it was alright for him. He'd been exercising his brain by singing karaoke in Dutch.

Still, it was just as well and soon he got us safely back. He shuffled off towards the bar while Hawkeye and I retired to our room.

Hawkeye went to relieve himself while I sat messing around with the telly. I couldn't seem to get a picture. I assumed it wasn't tuned in.

"What the *fuck* are you trying to do?"

Hawkeye stood there, zipping up.

"Trying to get some Dutch TV!"

"*You're* in no fit state for that! Give it here!"

He muscled in. He was just as useless as me. Still, not to be denied, I wandered off in search of help.

Up and down the stairs I went, along the corridors, getting lost. I couldn't find a soul to help. Then I must have passed out somewhere. I was lying on the floor. I got up in a dream-like state. I seemed to float back up to our room where Hawkeye lay asleep in bed.

I rapped away on the nearest door.

"Terry! Ted! Our tele's fucked! Come and help us twiddle our knobs!"

Nothing. No response at all.

Then I seemed to drift downstairs. Ted was propping up the bar.

"Where's Terry?"

"How should *I* know?"

"Well, he isn't in his room!"

"*Must* be."

"No, he's not, I've knocked!"

"Sure you got the right room?"

"Aye! On the left, next door to ours!"

"Tough! Piss-off back to bed!"

Suddenly I felt afraid, I don't know how and I don't know why, but deep confusion seemed to reign and it seemed essential that I found Terry. Why would he not answer the door? What the hell had happened to him? Ted had seemed a little flippant, what was he trying to hide from me?

I found myself outside in the street, throwing stones at Terry's window, or what I *thought* was Terry's window. Almost certainly it wasn't.

"TERRY! TERRY! WHAT'S THE MATTER? ARE YOU IN THERE? WHAT'S UP, PAL? . . . TERRY!!! . . . then I remembered our pact. Not to report any illness or injury.

That was it, I started to panic, I had gone completely mad. I turned and sprinted down the road, ending up at another hotel where I burst through the door, ranting and raving:

"HELP! HELP! THERE'S A GOOD MAN DOWN! HE COULD BE ILL OR EVEN WORSE! HE COULD BE LYING DEAD IN THERE! HE COULD'VE BEEN *MURDERED!!!* CALL THE POLICE!!!"

The woman behind the desk looked terrified, I could see her poor hands trembling. She was on the phone in a flash. The words 'murder' and 'English' were mentioned.

Then I snapped right out of it and suddenly it was no longer a dream. *Murder?* Had there been a *murder* and what was I doing in *this* hotel?

Soon enough the police turned up. Two of them and they looked *mean*. Both of them were carrying guns. Something strange was going on. Then it all came flooding back and everything fell into place. It all felt quite surreal, at first, but once I realised it had happened, all that I could feel was embarrassment. I crept out and hid in the bushes. The cops went off to *our* hotel. I followed at a discrete distance and finally slithered into the lobby. They were questioning Ted at the bar. His tone appeared to be one of annoyance. I slid past without being seen and made my way upstairs on tiptoe.

I awoke and wished I hadn't. My head was throbbing, mercilessly. Hawkeye was crashing about the room.

"Fuckin' hell man, settle down!"

"Hey," he said, "don't *you* give orders, Ted's just told me about last night!"

"That all happened?"

"Aye, it *did!*"

"Sorry, but I'm under stress!"

"Well pull yersell together, man! *No-one* needs *that* kind of drama! It's a holiday, remember? Let's not spoil what's left of it!"

And off he went to have some breakfast. I just lay there, suffering. He'd managed to get the TV on. Something, at least, appeared to be working.

Then a final night in the 'dam. The red light district beckoned us. The map came out for one last time and off we went in search of it.

"Look," said Hawkeye, "those three lasses!"

"*Those* three lasses, over there?"

"Aye."

"Well, there's only two, and those are blokes!"

Lasers were crap.

The streets meanwhile were full of people, punters, pimps, pushers, police; only a small proportion were female and they were always in twos or threes. We wandered around transfixed on the windows, some with velvet curtains drawn, others had a stool or a chair but always with a girl astride. *Wow,* I thought. *What a choice!* Everything was catered for. Different ages, shapes and sizes, fetishes, ethnicities. Their hair was black, brown, blonde, shades of red or crazy-coloured . . . long, short, afro, bald . . . anything that you could think of.

"Right then, Hawkeye, whaddya fancy?"

"All of 'em!" he offered, drooling.

"Off ya pop then, do the deed. Go and get yer gonads gooned!"

Yet he didn't, none of us did, if *one* had then the rest may have followed. Except for me. I was skint. I really didn't have the option.

There were lots of sex shops though and some of them were pretty grim. The videos got worse and worse:

"Lesbian Lust!"

"Fun with a Nun!"

"Teenage Orgy!"

"Dirty Dog!"

They even sold prosthetic arms! I stood there trying to work it out. Probably for amputees but what exactly was the sexual angle?

Finally we'd seen enough and headed back for farewell drinks, but not before we'd passed a canal that smelled like it was full of semen.

"Jesus fucking Christ!" coughed Ted. "That's the spunk of a thousand men!"

"You should know!" I offered, smugly.

Everyone laughed. All was forgiven.

The ferry back was like the first, except the whole thing was in daylight. Only one free meal this time but we'd already had our breakfast.

I had enough for one last pint. We sat there in the bar in silence. Something seemed to be bothering Ted. Finally he spat it out.

"I wonder," he began with hesitance, like he hadn't quite grasped the idea, "if *we* could be the first gang of lads to have *ever* visited Amsterdam *without* indulging in sex or drugs?"

None of us said anything, we all sat pondering the thought. It must have been a minute or two before he finally got a reaction.

Hawkeye smiled. Terry grinned. I began to chuckle a bit. Then we all just burst out laughing. Sadly, I'd laugh more that day than in the entire year that followed.

31

£20 a week was dire. I could barely feed myself. The sanction still had months to run, I had to sell some records, fast. I put an advert in the paper and got a fairly good response. I gave my address to the promising ones and barely had a few days passed when a couple of skinheads were sat on the carpet, browsing through a pile of singles. They were running a market stall and scanning all the discs in detail, separating good from bad, by *their* criteria, naturally. They gave me a price, a low one, so I turned them down and they upped it a bit. The only better deal they could offer was if they paid me half in dope. I took the cash, reluctantly, I hadn't a clue what dope was worth and I already had a bag of mushrooms, all that ganja wouldn't help if the drug squad crashed in through the door.

My birthday passed without celebration. Royal Mail still hadn't been in touch. The rumours seemed to be dying down. Perhaps nobody cared anymore? Though the future seemed uncertain I was in a better mood. If only I could survive the sanction, full-whack dole was on the horizon and possibly a training course. I'd struggle for a reference but at least I wouldn't be classed as a criminal. Tricky interviews lay ahead but who's to say I couldn't blag them?

Sadly, it was not to be. There was a knock on the door one morning. I'd been in the bath, relaxing. Soon I'd have to forget about that.

I opened the door to a middle-aged woman, smartly dressed but rather sombre.

"Mr Peagerm?"

"Aye, that's me."

This one wasn't from the God Squad.

"Come on in," I told her as I stood with just a towel around me. "Take a seat," I offered.

She declined. "No thanks, it won't take long."

She stood there with a pen and clip-board, glancing at me now and then, hastily explaining things while I just stood there in a trance. I was being charged, she said, under some old Section of some old Act, and I'd be appearing at Monkton Magistrates some time at the end of the month.

She ripped a charge sheet from her pad and planted it firmly into my hand. I had to sign for it, naturally, and then she said she'd need a description.

"Over six foot?"

"Six foot three."

"Brown eyes?"

"Aye. What's *this* for?"

"To make sure that it's *you* in Court."

"Can't you take a photo?"

"No."

Then she left me standing there. I could only stare at the charge sheet. It was suddenly real enough, they were going to make an example of me. *Of course* they were, they *always* were, you couldn't escape the wrath of Royal Mail. Any glimmer of hope had been crushed. The days were dark and depressing once more.

I made an appointment with a solicitor, Mr Michaelson, from Sedgeworth. All the locals used him though a few of them were sat in jail.

And there I sat in front of him. I decided he was Greek. Not that it made any difference, just an observation.

"Can I apply for Legal Aid?"

"Yes, of course you can," he said.

I filled out the appropriate forms.

"Right then, what can I do for you?"

I told him of my sorry tale as he sat there playing with his moustache. Then he scanned my ruffled charge sheet.

"So, you're pleading guilty to theft?"

"Well, *attempted* theft, really."

"All it says is 'theft' on here."

"Either way, it's all the same, except I never left the building."

"Ah, well, it's *not* the same. Not according to the law. A theft may not have taken place, you might just want to reconsider."

"But I gave them written statements, two confessions."

"That's irrelevant. British law is quite specific. I'm not sure that this is theft."

"So, you want me to trash my statements and get me off on a technicality?"

"I don't want a thing, my friend, it's *your* choice at the end of the day. I'm merely offering my opinion, how we proceed is up to you. There are no guarantees, of course, but *I* think that we have a case."

Then he clambered up from his seat and wandered around, scratching himself. There was plenty there to scratch. He sat back down and looked at me.

"Any previous convictions?"

"No, not really, a caution or two."

"What do you know about criminal records?"

I resisted the urge to be humorous.

"Well, since you're unemployed, what it means is, if convicted, legally you must declare it, each time an employer asks. This may last for many years, depending on the type of sentence. So, I shall ask you again. Are you *sure* you want to plead guilty?"

"Look," I said, "if I say 'no' and you succeed in getting me off, what's to stop a lesser charge, and if they nail me for that, what then? I'd look like a proper coward! No, I'm gonna tell the truth. They can judge me based on that. No more lying, no pretences."

He just sat there, stony-faced.

"Very well, it's your decision."

Only one thing left to ask.

"So, whaddya think I'll get?"

"It depends," he said with a sigh, "the Magistrates have *some* discretion. This is more a breach of trust than anything of monetary value. It depends what the lawyers demand, an absolute discharge is unlikely. So is a custodial sentence. Probably a fine, I'd say."

"You'll mitigate?"

"Of course we will, if not myself, perhaps Miss Hughes. I have another case to attend to. Either way, we'll do our best."

I left there feeling none the wiser, but at least I had representation. Court was a mere three weeks away. All that I could do was wait. The other case was soon apparent, one of Ted's old mates, a bouncer. He was up for GBH but *he* insisted he wasn't guilty. All the lads were loving it, predicting who'd get sent down first. Opinion swayed, this way and that. Justice, huh? It seemed like a lottery.

Waiting wasn't easy though, especially as I was skint. Music wasn't helping much, I'd sold the bulk of my record collection. Daytime telly? Well, forget it. It was far too cold for walks. The library was full of rubbish. Understanding, *that's* what I needed. So, I hit the bookies again, without any cash but a sense of purpose, watching, listening, asking questions, searching for enlightenment. Who *were* these people? Why were they gambling? Were they hooked, and if not, why not? How many lives would end up in turmoil? Surely it couldn't have been just mine? Mostly I was frowned upon, they didn't want their lives dissecting, especially by a fool like me who nobody could trust anymore. Still, it was pretty clear that most of them were losers, dreamers, wasting time and money and hope, lacking anything to aim for. How had *I* succumbed to this? I guessed I didn't have an off-switch, it had been the same with drinking, I was just a hopeless addict. Locked into the same routine, unable to resist those urges. I was understanding alright, pity it was all too late.

Meanwhile things were getting to me as pessimism crept in slowly, barely more than a week till Court and I was constantly on edge. *One last night on the tiles, perhaps?* Well, I wasn't eating much, so as I wasn't buying food then why not have a drink instead?

I was joined by Terry and Hawkeye, it was a Saturday afternoon, I lashed them down with a sense of purpose and everyone kept up with me.

"You'd better savour this," said Terry, "it may be *your* last drink for a while."

"Aye," said Hawkeye, "the last *real* one, it's jail-cell hooch from here on in! At least you'll have a sex life though! Fresh meat for the big lads, eh?"

"It's far more action than *you'll* ever see, ya ugly, pop-eyed, baldy get!"

This went on for quite a while until we all ran out of steam. A change of scenery was required. A taxi took us into Sedgeworth. We were drunk by eight o'clock. Terry was at the bar with a blonde. It looked like they were getting on. Some relation, obviously. Then I realised it was Caitlin, we had known her years ago, a little younger than all of us but a regular at local gigs.

"Caitlin!" I yelled. "Over here!"

She turned and smiled and came on over. She was with a friend called Jo. I thought I'd make some introductions.

"Alright Jo? My name's Eric. This is Hawkeye. You've met Terry?"

"Oh, I *have!*"

"A charmer, eh?"

Terry winked and staggered a bit.

"Caitlin, you look good but different. Is it the hair?"

"Perhaps," she said. "I've gone back to my natural tones."

She'd had it red, purple, all sorts.

"Well, it really suits you," I said. "The last I heard you were getting married?"

"No . . . that all fell apart."

"Sorry."

"Don't be, life's too short."

"Well, I think it *might* be for me."

"Why?"

"I'm up in Court next week. A minor indiscretion at work."

"Minor my arse!" Hawkeye suggested. "*We* all think he's up the creek, for all we know he could get life!"

Caitlin chuckled. "Oh I doubt it, Eric's daft but he's not *that* bad!"

"I'd hoped I might just get the sack, but no, they have to make an example. Anyway, I'm sure I'll manage . . ."

"Aye," said Terry, "you'll manage *some* things, but after a week or two in the clink, I doubt you'll manage a solid shite!"

I laughed it off . . . well, I had to, no point bringing the evening down, but Caitlin, what a ray of sunshine, maybe once all this was over I'd have the balls to ask her out? Obviously I *was* quite daft, I didn't have a job *or* prospects, still, even a friendly drink would be something to look forward to.

We all drank up and made for the door. Sedgeworth had a few more pubs, yet barely had we hit the street and Terry had poor Caitlin in tears. God knows what he'd said to her, the pair of them refused to say, but Terry did seem full of regret and decided he should head off home.

The rest of the night was a bit of a blur. All I remember was talking to Caitlin. Jo had disappeared at some point, scotching Hawkeye's hopes of a foursome. Maybe that was why she left? We ended up in a taxi regardless, pulling up at a little terrace, halfway up the hill from The Stag.

"*You* don't live in Trimley, Caitlin!"

"No. It's my mother's house. I'll see if she can drive me home."

Perhaps. Once we'd paid the fare.

We all sat rifling through our pockets, scrambling around for enough loose change. Things were spilling out all over, it was getting very messy. If we hadn't been so drunk it might have been embarrassing, but eventually we found enough and the driver left, shaking his head.

Caitlin knocked on her mother's door. Hawkeye and I just stood there, swaying.

"You can stay at mine," I said.

She knocked again, a little louder.

Still no answer.

"Got a phone?"

"Of course. All the modern amenities."

Not much food but what the hell. I couldn't let her freeze to death.

And off we went, it wasn't far, we managed it without much fuss, but when we got to the top of the stairs I didn't seem to have my keys.

Shit, I thought. *Not again?*

"What was the name of that taxi firm?"

"Why?"

"I think I dropped my keyring, when we tried to pay the bloke."

"Too late now, sort it tomorrow."

"Right then, back to *your* place, Hawkeye."

"*What?* Not a flippin' chance!"

"Come on man, we're freezing here!"

"Tough!"

Caitlin looked depressed.

Only one thing I could do.

"Stand back folks," I said with a sigh and, once again, I booted the door in.

On went the kettle and out came the cups while each in turn made use of the bathroom. Me and Hawkeye slumped on the couch while Caitlin tapped away on the phone.

Finally she got an answer. Not her mother, but her brother. Then they started arguing. He didn't want to drive her home.

"You nasty fucking little twat!"

She slammed the phone down, violently.

"No joy there?"

"Not with *him!* The selfish, slimy little bastard!"

"Look," I said, "*I'd* drive you home . . . if I hadn't lost my keys."

"And you're pissed!"

"Well, that too."

"It's fine," she said. "Mam's back soon."

Then she scrambled around in her handbag. "Oh . . . no, for fuck's sake, NO!"

"What?"

"I can't find *my* keys now! My cash card too . . . where's it gone?"

"No doubt on the floor of the taxi."

"Bollocks! Bollocks! Bloody bollocks!"

Ouch. "Haven't you got any spares?"

"Yes, inside the house! Have *you?*"

"Yes. Up at my parents' house."

"Well . . . I've got *cats* to feed!"

I thought about it for a moment.

"Want me to come and boot the door in?"

Then came tears. Floods of them. "Come here," I said and gave her a hug. "We'll get you in, the cats won't starve. Whatever we need to fix, we will."

"I know, I know, but it's a pain, and *that* little shit's upset me as well!"

"Aye, I know, but never mind," and I gave her a little kiss on the forehead.

Next I knew we were kissing for real, I grabbed her waist and pulled her in. We both fell backwards into Hawkeye. "*Jesus fuckin' Christ!*" he said. He leapt to his feet and made for the door as Caitlin and I got carried away, ripping at each other's clothes, heated, passionate, frenzied, drunk.

Then I suddenly pulled away.

"What's the matter?"

"I dunno. Something just came over me. I want this more than anything. But *now?* Well, maybe we shouldn't? You're upset and I've been stressed. Something doesn't feel quite right. Perhaps I want to savour it?"

It may have been that, despite the ripping, neither of us had removed any clothes. Caitlin had a shoulder out but otherwise was fully dressed.

"Right," she told me, getting up. "I'll try this bloody phone again."

I sat there having second thoughts. That ruffled look was really hot.

"Hello? Mam?"

And that was it. She was gone in less than a minute. She kissed me as she disappeared, but not before she'd left her number.

I just sat and stared at it, enthralled by all that lovely writing. Wow, what a girl, I thought, and somehow I'd just let her go! But maybe, once I'd been to Court, I'd call her and we'd work it out. I wasn't much of a catch, of course, but here I was, I had her number, who could say what lay ahead?

I woke up feeling pretty bad. Sickly, nauseous, all that stuff. I fixed the door as best as I could then tramped up to my parents' house in order to retrieve my keys.

My younger brother answered the door.

"Whatcha want?"

"Just my keys."

"Drunk again?"

"Well, it happens."

"True."

"So . . . anything new?"

There wasn't much, there rarely was, he didn't ask a thing about me. Could it be they *still* never knew? Perhaps they wanted *me* to tell them? Mam and Dad were both back home, my elder sister lived elsewhere. Two of them were worriers, the other two I couldn't read.

Later I gave Caitlin a call. No sense leaving it a week. She'd been on my mind all day. Eventually, she answered me.

"So, you're in?"

"Obviously. Smashed the back door glass with a hammer. Mam said I should get a locksmith. On a Sunday? Glass is cheaper. Sat up drinking wine all night . . ."

"Should've rang me up, for company."

185

"You'd have been asleep by then. Did you manage to get undressed?"

"No."

"Didn't think you would."

Then she gave the sweetest chuckle.

"You remember?"

"Yes, of course. Still, I'm surprised *you* do!"

"You were shining, like an angel!"

"Yeah, right!"

"*Of course* you were, but come on Caitlin, really though, it wouldn't have been a night to remember. Look, fancy a drink on Thursday? Just a couple, nothing heavy. I'm in Court on Friday morning. Help me calm my nerves a bit."

She agreed. That felt good. Something to look forward to. As long as the bastards didn't nail me, there was hope, there really was.

I thought about her all week long and cursed myself for all my failings. Still, I could start anew and what if Caitlin were the catalyst? She was studying, why not me? I was barely into my thirties. I could do it. Sure I could. All I needed was a reason.

I took time one afternoon to write a letter to my parents. Then I dropped it off at Terry's with strict instructions to deliver it should I fail to return from Court. All apologies, basically. Hard to explain the whys and wherefores. If they didn't lock me up I'd spill my guts, face to face, before the papers blurted it out.

Then, eventually, it was Thursday. Caitlin met me back in Sedgeworth. She looked stunning and I was sober. I could hardly believe my luck. We chatted away, at length, all night, the talk was easy, natural. She told me all about college, her cats and spoke with a warmth that pulled you in. I said I needed a brand new start. Uni perhaps. She told me to go for it. We were out till the last bus home, we talked so much we lost track of time and ended up having to run to catch it.

It was just the same on the bus, except that we were sitting closer. Not much eye contact this time, but when we did exchange the odd glance the sudden tension was almost unbearable.

My stop was a while before hers. She kissed me as the bus approached. Time stood still as I closed my eyes. It was torture getting off.

I lay awake in bed that night. Little hope of any sleep. Suddenly the telephone rang. I scrambled up to answer it.

"*HEY! THIS IS MR BIG! YOUR ANUS IS IN SERIOUS DANGER!*"

"Oooh!" I said before slamming it down.

It would be a long old night.

32

Feb. 28th. Judgement Day. I ran a bath and had a shave. I dressed as smartly as I could then drove the car to Monkton.

I sat there in the courtroom foyer, folks were streaming in and out. Lots of youngsters, laughing and joking. I was in and out of the toilet. Finally, Miss Hughes arrived. She looked pretty good to me. Smart and stylish, very professional. Maybe I just had a chance? She smiled as she reviewed her notes. *Yes. Right. Uh huh. Of course.* Then she went through Court procedures and later I was led inside.

I had to stand before the bench as someone read the charges out. They echoed through the empty space. I was feeling quite detached. I looked at all three Magistrates, an elderly woman was sat in the centre, flanked by a couple of middle-aged men, they all looked *very* serious.

Miss Hughes was sitting to my right, the Prosecution next to her. A tall, dark and handsome type. *Be nice to her, be nice to ME.* I'd hoped that things would speed along. After all, I was guilty. Not a chance, you had to suffer. The Magistrate in chief addressed me.

"Would you like to be tried with a jury?"

Crown Court? Certainly not! All those silly wigs and stuff? I was forced to decline *that* offer. I had seen *Twelve Angry Men* and Hawkeye had done jury service. Crown Court was a lottery and I didn't intend to buy a ticket.

Then the Prosecution stood, the charges were read out in detail. Evidence was on display, the envelope that I had 'stolen'.

I was asked to enter a plea.

"Guilty," I said, ashamedly.

Then it was time for the mitigation. Miss Hughes slowly got to her feet.

She began by clearing her throat, a silence descended on the courtroom. Time appeared to be standing still . . . "Mr Peagerm is . . ." she started.

She was reading from her notes, pretty badly in *my* opinion, stuttering in a monotone voice, and weakly, like a scared little girl! My heart sank, I was done for, where was the drama, where was the passion? The whole thing sounded like a sham, I sat there stunned in disbelief. She should've been strutting around the courtroom, clasping her lapels with authority, pitying that poor wretch in the dock who, judging by his sorry tale, was obviously a victim of circumstance! She was letting me down, big style, as the Magistrates looked on, expressionless. Clearly they were not impressed. I found it hard to believe myself! Perhaps the Prosecution had got to her, it was mind games after all, that poor Miss Hughes, so inexperienced, lambs to the slaughter, the pair of us!

Once she'd hammered the last nail in, the Prosecution stood back up. He was asked for further comments. He suggested *I* pay costs. Oh, *very* nice, I thought. Kick a fella when he's down. I got twenty quid a week and *still* they wanted their pound of flesh.

The Magistrates then left the room. It was bad but just *how* bad? I was feeling rather numb.

Finally, they reappeared.

Six months probation, nothing to pay. I gave an enormous sigh of relief. Somehow, I'd retained my freedom, they could pay their own damn costs! I turned around and thanked Miss Hughes, for what exactly, I dunno, then quickly made my way outside and filled my lungs with a breath of fresh air.

Everything looked beautiful, the sky, the trees, the shops, the people; even the smoke from the chemical plants looked quite poetic from a distance. True, I had a minor conviction and that would still upset some folk, but I was merely Eric Peagerm, human, fallible, small-time thief.

I found the car and drove away. The traffic seemed much kinder than usual. I was so relaxed and relieved I didn't even feel like a drink. And then of course there was Caitlin to think of. She was my reward for the truth. Would she feel as happy as *I* did? Hope so, I thought, I really do. I looked in the mirror and saw her reflection. All the birds were singing her name. I drove towards her, getting closer. I drove into the sun, she was there. She was *everywhere*.